What a Next of Kin!

What a Next of Kin!

Charles Alobwed'Epie

Langaa Research & Publishing CIG
Mankon, Bamenda

Publisher:
Langaa RPCIG
Langaa Research & Publishing Common Initiative Group
P.O. Box 902 Mankon
Bamenda
North West Region
Cameroon
Langaagrp@gmail.com
www.langaa-rpcig.net

Distributed outside N. America by African Books
Collective
orders@africanbookscollective.com
www.africanbookscollective.com

Distributed in N. America by Michigan State
University Press
msupress@msu.edu
www.msupress.msu.edu

ISBN: 9956-616-62-1

DISCLAIMER

The names, characters, places and incidents in this book are either the product of the author's imagination or are used fictitiously. Accordingly, any resemblance to actual persons, living or dead, events, or locales is entirely one of incredible coincidence.

Contents

Chapter One

As usual in the evening Mr. Ndi sat in his veranda singing one of his lachrymose songs that made him sigh and sigh until he went to bed in disgust. That day he turned and saw his eldest daughter enter the house with a shopping bag. She had done the last shopping before the D day. He eyed her with mixed feelings – half admiringly and half disdainfully and shook his head. She was a pearl of unearthly beauty – tall, black and stately. She was in fact a replica of her mother, a woman he had loved beyond description, but a woman who died in childbirth leaving behind that proverbial beauty.

He recalled how he had taken the child to Shishong orphanage and after years of missionary expertise and devotion the Reverend Sisters had made the child survive. He was then invited to come for the child. He went for her and after paying a negligible amount, he was given the child.

Now Emma (Immaculate), as he fondly called her was preparing for marriage and would very soon become some other person's property. "Oh, that she were a boy!" he exclaimed in his heart and sighed. Gall jetted into his mouth. He spat out what he could and swallowed what he could not. A chill ran through him as he thought if he had known that his first wife's witchery would render his future so bleak, he would have killed her when he first suspected that she was responsible for his misfortunes. He remembered vividly how after years of a childless marriage he had sought her approval before getting married to his late second wife. He was then a 'head-man' at the CDC rubber plantation in Tiko.

And it was only by virtue of his working down south, especially as head-man that a pearl of such beauty accepted to marry him.

His first wife had tended not to be worried about her co-wife. Because the CDC houses for the plantation-hands were extremely small, she surrendered her bedroom to her co-wife and accepted her husband to make for her a portable bed that could be set up in the evening and dismantled in the morning in the parlour. Ndi was very thankful for that magnanimity. They lived together harmoniously so to speak, and very soon, the second wife got pregnant. But then, disaster struck at childbirth.

After the death of his second wife, Ndi swore never to marry again. In 1959 however, the KNDP won elections in Southern Cameroons and his uncle was made Secretary of State in charge of Public Works (SSPW). The SSPW appointed Ndi to the lucrative post of Storekeeper General in charge of the Tiko Wharf warehouses. With that, Ndi automatically became the overseer of most government sponsored building projects. In 1960, he visited the Kumba Eastern Council bridge-building projects and spent two months in Bakossiland. When he returned from there he opened two large hardware stores in Muyuka and Kumba. Before long, he expanded business all over the Southern Cameroons and thus became chief supplier of building and road construction materials to most private and government building companies. Money started pouring in. And once money started pouring in, it became incumbent on him to marry for the third time. But before he took in another wife, he moved house from the slums of the CDC plantation-hands to Likumba Senior Service Quarter, where he bought a five bedroom house with a sizeable veranda.

As usual, his first wife approved of the marriage and facilitated its consummation especially as the new building was ample enough to provide independent rooms for each of the wives, guests and children. Ndi was very thankful to her once again. His third wife soon took in and begot a daughter. To appreciate his first wife's openness and devotion, he named the child after her. He called the child Mafor, a name he fondly shortened to Mma.

He and his two wives tended to live happily and harmoniously. But then, something kept gnawing at the root of his heart. With money flowing in and the acquisition of landed and other properties, he needed a boy – a next of kin. And so, he forced his third wife to wean the child at three months. He thought if the Reverend Sisters could make the first daughter survive on canned milk, then of course they would, with money pouring in, be able to make the child survive on canned milk and foods. And so, in the fifth month of the first delivery, his third wife took in again. And that became routine. After his wife had given birth to the sixth daughter, Ndi decided to consult a soothsayer on why he could not be blessed with a boy.

"Fai Nchotu, I am sitting on hot coals. As you see me, I am advancing in age but I have not got a next of kin or what we call *chopchair*. My third wife is on her sixth daughter and I am getting very worried about her ability to beget me a son. At this age, I don't think getting another wife to bear me a son is ideal. Such a wife could even beget a son, but he wouldn't be my blood. What do the stars say about me? And how can I overcome it?" Ndi asked with a lugubriousness that told Fai Nchotu his sad tale.

"How many wives have you?" Fai asked.

"I have two. I have been married thrice. My first wife has no child. My second wife died in childbirth leaving me with a daughter. My third wife is my worry now. She has begotten six daughters," Ndi responded, his voice sinking with bitterness in his throat.

"Are your two wives living together with you?" Fai Nchotu asked with a voice chagrined with ill-omen.

"Yes," Ndi responded sharply.

"You see, ignorance is the base of your problems. A human being is body and soul but you are only body. By this I mean, you do not know the working of the night. Your first wife is your husband and you are her wife. She is responsible for all that is happening to you. As you see her, she is a queen in the spirit world. She is the queen of the second most powerful spirit Beelzebub and she has got eleven children, all boys, in the spirit world. That is why she cannot bear children in this physical world. So long, as she is with you, nothing good in terms of human beings can come your way. Your daughters who get married will beget sons and daughters but those who remain in your house will only beget daughters. Wait a minute; you say you have seven daughters, but I see you have eight children with a son amongst them. You have got a son. You have eight children. Yes, you have," Fai Nchotu said emphatically and choked.

"I have not got a son anywhere. I have not," Ndi responded confusedly and disappointedly with the twist.

"If you say you have got no son anywhere then I would say we call off this consultation. You return and come some other day. It may be I need to propitiate my spirits for a better insight into their world," Fai said and folded up his divining apparatus.

Ndi felt the spikes of the sudden end of the consultation devastate his soul. He asked himself why Fai was so categorical about his having a son. His mind combed all the nooks and crannies of Tiko especially around Likumba; Mutengene, Buea, Victoria, and even Kumba but found nowhere, no woman with whom he would have had a son. When he was a CDC plantation-hand, the strain of work and the meagre wages kept him within the confines of his house. Thus he couldn't go out to amuse himself with other women. When he became Storekeeper General and money

4

started pouring in, the desire to horde money and acquire landed and other properties and thus become a force to reckon with, overshadowed every other pleasure. It was routine for him to leave work and either go buying property or return home. Thus he was extremely faithful to his childbearing wife. He pulled out a one pound note, placed it on the table and bade Fai Nchotu good bye.

Chapter Two

Ndi left Fai Nchotu with a throbbing headache. Time and again he mumbled that all divinations go cripple. He wondered why a divination that was going on so well got an unexpected twist – a faulty and sour turn towards the end. He put two and two together and at last concluded that if his first wife were truly queen Beelzebub, it meant she could eavesdrop on conversations no matter where. As queen of the second most powerful spirit, distance and obstacles did not exist. So, she might have overheard the revelations Fai Nchotu was making against her and counteracted by infusing false images in his divining apparatus. But then, he thought again, Fai might have simply misinterpreted genuine images. "What if he meant that I shall have a son? Haven't I heard that sometimes images get blurred and are badly interpreted by the seers? For sure, Fai will get it right the next time," Ndi concluded and thought of returning to him in the near future. And though his last daughter was only three months old, he thought it would be good to wean her and start looking for the envisaged boy.

Ndi returned home distraught with the way he had to approach his dilemma. If he manifested any overt hostility against his first wife that could create an unfavourable atmosphere in his attempt to woo his third wife into accepting to wean the three-months-old daughter that night. He remembered how resistant she had been in the last two untimely weaning. She had to be; because in the two last pregnancies, she was virtually ostracized by women groups in Likumba. They criticized her in her face and composed derogatory songs against her. In the last pregnancy, she could not bear it. So, she moved town. She went to Mundemba shortly after realizing that she was pregnant again and stayed there till she gave birth. Ndi knew it would be a tough fight that would require the intervention of his first wife; so he played down his anger against her. He got home and for the first time, pampered his daughters to the admiration of their mother.

"Joe," his third wife called admiringly. "I believe something is either very seriously wrong today, or very seriously right. For the first time I see the glow of fatherly love shrouding my children. I believe the children are seeing a different father in you today. Whenever you return from work frowning you scare them away and make them lose the paternal touch they need to grow up well."

"It is fantastic today. How I wish it remained like that! But Joe was not like that. It may be the pressure of work. I believe we are now moving into a new era," the first wife interjected."

"I don't think I frown for nothing. The two of you treat me badly. When I am away, you connive to maltreat me. When I go to you, my first wife, you send me off with the flick of the finger to my third wife who always has an excuse for not wanting me. And who can be happy with people who are not happy with him?" Ndi feigned an angry response while curdling his daughters.

"Who drives you away? If you are advised and restrained from being a fowl, you say you are driven away? Tell me; in the whole of Tiko especially here in Likumba, Mutengene, Victoria, Buea where else have you seen a woman laying children as I lay? Isn't it shameful that wherever I go I carry the mark and ruin of regular childbirth?" the third wife asked with a voice irked with anger.

"Don't lose your bearings. Your remarks have led to all this. And once more, I believe I have to marry another woman who can want me. The two of you have spited me and I need not pretend that I have a wife in either of you. If you play, I shall abandon this house to the two of you," Ndi said emphatically.

"Yes, I predicted it. That is how you start. That is your snare, pretext to pamper children. This time you will not have your way. You can abandon the house or go and marry another hen. Look at me, which of my age mates has this type of flabby stomach – a stomach battered and eroded out of shape by constant childbearing?" the third wife asked with raging anger.

Ndi looked at her. Behind the ruined features he could still decipher traces of lost beauty. He got up and defying her anger, stretched himself and went to her room. He pulled off his coat and hung it in the wardrobe. The third wife dashed into the room to see what he was doing. She saw the coat hung in the wardrobe. She dragged it out violently from the wardrobe and carried it to the sitting room and threw it on a chair. Ndi got the coat and took it to the room again and hung it on a nail in the wall. The third wife got it once more and threw it half way on the chair. It rolled down and fell on the ground.

"OK, you have given me the go ahead," Ndi said rather confusedly.

"You are not even ashamed of yourself. Since when did you move room? I have given you both the go ahead and the go behind," the third wife rebuked.

"OK, we shall see who is who in this house." Ndi said threateningly and sat down in the parlour, placing both legs on the parlour table.

"The door is opened," the third wife responded sharply.

"For me to marry a fourth wife?" he asked.

"Even a fifth, sixth, seventh to what you like. This is your first wife. Go to her room. Did she tell you she does not need a man?" the third wife asked.

"OK," Ndi mumbled, stretched himself on the chair, adjusted his sitting position and soon snored away.

His third wife bathed the children and after feeding them and getting them to bed, went into her room, locked the door and pushed the bed against it to block and prevent any intrusion.

In the morning Ndi discovered he had spent the night in the parlour. Anger welled up in him. He got up tidied himself up and left for work. In the evening, he returned with sordid folds of anger in his face. He did not greet his wives but went straight and sat in his veranda and sang his sorrows to himself. Thus in the midst of abundance Ndi became a singer of lachrymose songs.

Chapter Three

His first daughter had been married for three years. She had begotten a son and was expecting another child. It may be another son. Ndi remembered he had urged Mma not to marry. If she were not married her son would be his *chop chair*. But as the saying goes, breasts cover the heart of the woman and prevent the sun's rays from reaching it and so she does not reason. "What pleasure did Mma find in a husband that she would not have found in a boyfriend? Aren't there thousands of boys, poor boys ready to impregnate wealthy girls for free?" Ndi asked himself and sighed. "Let her go on begetting male children in her husband's house. After all, even if she remained here to have the sons, they would not have been my blood. They would have been some other persons' blood, and that would not have been different from the reality before me, namely, that this wealth shall be inherited by a person who is not of my first degree blood." Ndi grumbled, screwed his face, spat and tried to think of something else – some other distraction. But what else? What else in the face of the amassed property? What else could Ndi think of? There was a Bamenda Prime Minister, there were Bamenda Secretaries of State but none was as rich as he was. What else could he be thinking about but a next of kin? Was he to become a dog that huts for its master? For whom was he hunting? As these sordid thoughts gnawed at his heart he remembered what Fai Nchotu had told him. Fai had told him that his married daughters would beget sons and daughters but the unmarried ones would beget only

11

daughters. So even if Mma had accepted to remain unmarried and beget him children, they would not have been sons. That meant that there was the working of the devil in relation to having sons in his family. So it was necessary for him to return to Fai Nchotu and discuss about the son he was talking about.

One Saturday evening, he went to consult him. Fai saw him and laughed. "A dog does not shun a bone," he said as he offered Ndi a chair. "Welcome. Sit down and tell me if you have come to terms with yourself. Have you now accepted that a son is amongst your children?" Fai asked smiling.

"It may be the one to come. I have combed the universe but don't see where I have, would have had or may have. My childbearing wife has refused weaning the child so how do I have…?" Ndi asked.

"OK, if you say you don't have, I need not belabour the point. 'A good turn does not miss its way', if it is yours, you will get it," Fai said.

"Yes, but a good turn can be misdirected. I am very confused with my situation. You say my first wife is responsible for my undoing. Though I have no cause to reproach her, I feel eh, eh, eh…"

"Your first wife, as I have said is a queen in the spirit world. She took human form as a sort of holiday – a transitional period within her life cycle. That is what great spirits do. They change forms; they take on new forms to enjoy the different opportunities offered by a desired form. Your first wife is the queen of wealth. She brought you all the wealth you have. Look at it this way, in the whole of Southern Cameroon, you are the richest person. How comes that whatever you touch turns into wealth? That wealth is mystical and cannot be made to be inherited by a permanent figure – a son. It must dissipate upon the death of your first wife. She will return with it and you will die a wretch as you were before the KNDP victory at the elections. She influenced the evolution of Southern Cameroon to suit her qualms. And when she is fed up and decides to return to her royalty, all of you who are enjoying power and glory now, will sink into the abyss of infirmity, you will lose fame and be derided by the people you now look low upon. Verily, verily, I tell you, the very colts you ride now and flowers are thrown on their path will throw you down in rebellion. You will die and be buried with less glory." Fai predicted ominously.

Ndi heard a million insect chirps, a billion rattles, massed nondescript sounds in his ears. He trembled. Sweat sprouted on his body. He lost touch with reality. When he recovered, he drew his nose and asked, "Then what is the use of wealth?"

"It is a pastime, a false determiner of protocol and that is all. In reality it means nothing. Wealth means nothing. You see, it is an inconvenience man toils for, for nothing, and takes pleasure in toiling for it, for nothing. Ask him to define it, and you will hear him stammer. He stammers because he does not know what it really is. In spite of that, since it is in the sway of Beelzebub it can't be dismissed with the flick of the finger. For sure, wealth cannot be dismissed with the flick of the finger. It must mean something. But what? What does it mean? A dark veil with the vague words 'human nature', shroud its definition. And like human nature, wealth has many definitions. People who define it in terms of money and property narrow down what it really is. You see, within our small sphere, we are limited in knowing what wealth is and what we are looking for, in it. See it this way Mr. Ndi, a person gets very rich as you are and instead of making the best use of his wealth, he starts looking for a son to inherit the wealth. Of course, his son in due course would also look for a son to inherit the wealth and the vicious cycle goes on. Can we therefore define wealth as something that is of no use to its owner and of use only to his sons? What a contradiction! What reminiscence of a coffin! No matter how beautiful a coffin is, it's of no use to its weird occupant. It's proverbial only to the on-lookers, the main bereaved, his immediate family members, and the admiring praise-singing mourners. That is all. What a shame to the craftsman who stretches his ingenuity beyond measure, conceives the design of a coffin and executes its production with exquisite dexterity for the admiration of arrogant and hypocritical mourners! Can sons who know they are inheriting great wealth actually mourn? Are sons born only to inherit property? Is wealth something that we discard to sons? If so, can't sons become wealthy without inheriting? From whom did you inherit, Mr. Ndi?"

"What is the best use of wealth then? How can somebody say he is wealthy if he has no next of kin? Should people not possess wealth simply because it is reminiscent of coffins? Wealth is the opposite of poverty. And poverty is that gnawing, degrading downright cruel and graceless, sordid and miserable state of being nobody wants to be associated with. Wasn't it that he who was given five thousand gold coins increased them by five thousand and proudly welcomed his master with the good news? And he who was given two thousand increased them by two thousand and also welcomed his master proudly with the good news? But he who was given one thousand buried them and yielded nothing and welcomed his master with foul talk? Isn't it therefore clean and clear that unproductively that breeds poverty breeds evil? Wealth cannot be what every Dick and Harry can possess. It cannot be the seed that falls by the road side for uncouth birds to eat. It can't be sown on rocky ground where it wouldn't take root. It must be sown on fertile soil for it to germinate, grow and yield fruit. That fertile ground is a male heir, insurer of continuity. Surely, a male heir. Nothing short of that. A male heir, undisputed first degree blood, icon of self, keeper of the homestead. I can't understand why you don't see it that way. I would want you to tell me why I can't beget a son."

"Your problem is simple. Your first wife converts your son-bearing sperms into daughter-bearing ones and there is nothing you can do about it. A woman is a receptacle. Whatever you put in it, it retains. She does not change it of her own prowess. Garbage in, garbage out. All women are capable of son-bearing but if the astral world changes the sperm why should you blame the woman? Put yourself in your first wife's place. She brought you wealth in order to enjoy it with you. But because of her nature, she cannot bear you children, not to talk of sons. Now because of your nature, you are looking for a son to inherit her wealth. If you were her how would you feel? And how would you react?"

Ndi's ears hummed. The world whirled with him. He felt as if he had fallen in a barbed wired fence with the spikes tearing his flesh. Gall oozed into his mouth. He breathed torturously and hit the blank – collapsed. Fai Nchotu laughed and tapped him on the back.

"Don't kill yourself. Don't faint for nothing. You have a son. You are not like other people. For sure, you have a son and for his sake, your first wife shall not take her wealth with her when she decides to return to her royalty. Spirits don't die, they slough – they transform. Be glad and make merry. Your son will make you whole. Your name shall not be lost. It shall reign for a long, long time even after your death. Be blessed. Go in the peace of the lord."

Chapter Four

Ndi left Fai Nchotu with a sore heart. He was once again disappointed with his divination. He wondered how on earth a traditional seer would end a divination as if it were a pastor's sermon. There were parts of it that were quite interesting but most of it was questionable. When he got home, he took solace in singing his wailing songs at his veranda. So he got his sofa and sat down and while he sang, his first wife brought him his delicacy – ground nuts from home. He eyed them with mixed feelings, sighed and abandoned them where she put them. When she thought he might have finished eating, she came in to collect the container. On finding it still untouched she remarked, "I have observed with disheartening concern that you have generalized your disagreement with your wife. You have extended it to all, even the children of the house. You carry a scrofulous face all around as if we advised her not to yield to your demand…"

"Shut up, you principality of the highest order, devil incarnate, source of my doom. You thought I won't know your mission. I know. I know. Open your cursed mouth again and you will go parking to return to your royalty. Open your evil mouth again – shit, beef," Ndi insulted, took an ominous step toward her and thinking she would be frightened and run away, threw a ferocious slap at her. Poor third wife! She did not expect an onslaught as a recompense for her generosity – offering her husband *country* groundnuts. And thinking it was a feigned attack, she did not duck to avoid the slap. It homed in squarely with a deafening bang on her

17

left jaw, causing a couple of teeth to fly out of her mouth. She stood transfixed as the effect of the slap coursed through her making her look shrunken and terribly sick. Then she fell limply straightforward, the way a scarecrow falls, without struggle. Ndi might not have expected that outcome. But in order not to show cowardice, he kicked her a couple of times. The children yelled in disbelief and fright.

The third wife heard the yell and rushed to the scene. "What are you doing – getting mad?" she asked, and without thought, and perhaps under the spell of years of built in grudges and urge for revenge, gathered every bit of her strength together, and probably assisted by some weird hand seized Ndi midway, yanked him upward, spun with him a couple of times and let go, the manner a weight-thrower lets go the weight. Ndi flew in the air a good number of meters away and fell with a thump and remained motionless where he fell. "You this he-goat, you want to kill an innocent old woman? Come again and touch her and you will see me squeeze your breath out of your lungs. Stupid," she threatened and insulted. On second thought however, and fearing counterattack, she rushed into the kitchen and took a pestle, then stood guard like a Roman Centurion over her 'fallen' co-wife waiting for Ndi. After what appeared to be too long a wait, she felt an upsurge of concern and regret take possession of her. She exhaled noisily like a deflating balloon and dashed forth to find out why Ndi was not reacting. To her horror she saw the unthinkable.

Ndi's face was frightfully pale and elongated by the impact of the fall; his eyes bulged, and his mouth, wide open, gave the impression of an obscene yawn, or a desired but unrealized appeal for help – unrealized by the sudden loss of memory. The third wife shivered with fright. She had not heard him groan nor ask for help. She had simply seen him remain motionless where he had fallen. And mistaking that for male prowess thought of re-enforcing their defence by going for the pestle. Furthermore she could not believe that her tender and frail hands could inflict any remarkable hurt on Ndi. But then, there was the reality. Ndi cast a blank beady stare at her like a dead fish.

Over taken by grief and concern, she called her first daughter and asked her to go and call their neighbour, Mr. Ndeb. He came promptly and on seeing Ndi's state asked what had happened. "He, he f, f, f, fell, he fell," the third wife bumbled. "Let's send for an ambulance. He has to be rushed to hospital. His pulse is very low," Mr. Ndeb said emphatically. Presently, the ambulance arrived and Ndi was rushed to hospital.

Chapter Five

The reanimation ward staff went to work immediately. They asked the third wife what had happened. She stammered glumly. They abandoned her and followed medical procedure under such circumstances. After two hours of hard work, Ndi regain consciousness.

"Madam," the nurse called her attention. "We need your cooperation. You seem to be too aggrieved and unable to answer questions. That won't help. You must take courage. Though he has regained consciousness he can't be of help now. We can only rely on you. We need to know what happened to him. So far we have examined his skull but there seems to be nothing wrong with it. So tell us what happened," the nurse insisted.

"It is he who started it. I pushed him and he fell with the buttocks," the third wife responded.

"*A ha*! No doubt you are maudlin. I suspected a fight and thought somebody had hit him with a club on the head. OK, fine. We shall have to X-ray his vertebral column. After the X-ray, we shall move him to the ward. Which ward would you like him hospitalized?" the nurse asked.

"The Senior Service Ward (SSW)," she responded.

"Are you sure you will be able to pay for the SSW? OK, fine. Go to that office and get the prescription. When you pay, bring the receipts here and show them to any nurse you meet here."

The third wife did as she was told to do and brought the receipts. Ndi was X-rayed and after that, he was taken to the SSW. The next day, the results of the X-ray showed that he had a fractured vertebral column with three slipped discs. He thus needed a complex operation to re-arrange the discs. In an operation of that magnitude, the matron usually counselled the patient to make a will if they had not done so; ask for blood donors; and finally, be baptized or be reconciled with God if they had not been practicing Christians or Moslems. In the evening the matron went to counsel Ndi.

Once he heard about making a will, he grew limp and furious. His blood pressure shot up. He knew making a will was tantamount to declaring the next of kin. Who would be his next of kin – his third wife who had 'killed' him, or his eldest daughter who was already married, or any of the other remaining daughters, or his first wife, the devil incarnate?

"I shall like to be operated without making a will matron," he said in a hiccough.

"It is necessary to make a will. We insist on that not because we expect any bad outcome but because it is our routine – normal medical routine."

"I have no will to make. I have no heir. If death comes, let it take me. Let it take me. I am making no will. You can even stop the operation. Can't I be treated without an operation? People sustain broken waists in the villages and get well through herbal treatment and massaging. I prefer that."

"Mr. Ndi, people who go through that process of healing live very miserable lives – lives of incessant pain and anxiety. The spine is a very delicate part of the body. A little bit of negligence can lead to devastating paralysis. So, people should not play with it. The fact that you are in the SSW shows that you are a man of substance. That is your wife. I can call her if you like. She can be your next of kin. Do you say you don't have children or relatives to be your next of kin? I don't understand you. It is generally prudent to make a will before one is anesthetized."

"Your suggestion is ominous and riles me. It makes me worried. Is a will an operation knife? Are people unable to make wills not operated upon?"

"OK, let's not make a botched job of the whole thing. You will undergo the operation without making a will."

The next morning two specialists operated Ndi. It was a long delicate and tasking operation. The doctors were delighted that he did not bleed much and that everything went on according to plan. They gave him a fifty, fifty chance of full recovery. The matron paid special attention to him and always assigned two nurses to take care of him. He recovered steadily and within three weeks they could raise him to a partial sitting position.

One day, the matron noticed that the presence of his third wife tended to raise his ire. No matter how convivial he was in her absence, once she entered the ward, he turned crusty. "Mr. Ndi," the matron addressed him. "I have observed with dismay that you don't talk to your wife. Whenever she sets foot in this ward you turn your back against her. When she greets you, you never respond. I believe she is conscious of it and that is why she squirms when coming in or going out of the ward. The two of you are being gnawed by innate guilt. That of course, affects me because I feel I failed in my duty to reconcile you before the operation. I should have insisted that you reconcile with God and man before that operation. Your wife confessed that she pushed you and you got hurt. A wife does not push a husband in vain. There should be a reason. Now that you are recovering, please, reconcile with all around you. We are lucky you survived the operation. Just imagine, (God forbid) that all did not go on well, just think of the sordid way you would have met your Lord and God."

"Matron, I respect you very much and would have readily done what you are saying. But how can I reconcile with my first wife who has deprived me of an heir? How can I reconcile with my third wife for whom I challenged principalities but whose recompense is my physical undoing? Am I sure I can ever be a man again? You assure me the operation went well and the doctors are optimistic, but time and again my lower limbs die or go numbed for hours. My life is now in the balance, and should I go excusing people who are responsible for my ruination? Matron, what is in the 'stomach' does not smell until it is either farted or spoken. My disposition to forgive is dependent on my recovery – full recovery."

"That doesn't speak well of a Christian. Didn't Christ say, 'Father forgive them because they know not what they are doing?' And wasn't it on the cross where he suffered pain that he forgave his executioners? You will better reconsider your stand. Quick and sound recovery depends on a sound mind – a healthy mind in a healthy body and vice versa. Cleanse your heart of impurities and all other things will be well with you."

"Matron, I believe if you were to exchange places with me, you would not be saying what you are saying. Nobody goes sowing for birds to eat. Nobody goes sowing on rocky soil. People sow on fertile soil for good harvest. And when the harvesting is done, it is stored and protected to feed the farmer's progeny."

"That is true Mr. Ndi. But it is not as simplistic as that. Grudge and hardheartedness may worsen your state. I don't know the harm your first wife inflicted on you but I believe she would be repentant and apologetic if she knew she had hurt you. So, be sure you are not blaming and, so to speak, punishing an ignorant innocent woman."

"Matron, it is he who sleeps in a house who knows the hole in the wall that announces daybreak."

Chapter Six

The matron's advice set Ndi drifting into total chaos. He could neither keep awake without worries nor sleep conveniently. When awake, he was tormented by the thought of several things – his wealth, recovery, death, heir and the matron's advice. When he tried to sleep, he became a victim of snoozes interlaced with nightmares. This was worsened by the placement of his ward – one of the last rooms of a six single bedroom ward.

The four buildings housing the Senior Service Wards were built a good distance away from the hum and buzz of the common people's wards. Each of the first three buildings (known as the intermediate wards) was a six bedroom structure with two beds in each room, and the last one was a six bedroom structure (the real SSW) with only one bed in a room. The buildings were spread on two hectares of land called Crystal Gardens. And as one can conjecture, the name is suggestive of splendour. And really, Crystal Gardens was splendid. Its magnificent lawns laced with assorted luxuriant flowers, shaded by flowery trees and lianas gave it a cool conducive atmosphere for recovery. The buildings were interconnected with a fantastic network of wide external corridors meant to ease movement from ward to ward even in the raining season. The corridors served also as recreational ground for recovering patients. There, they learnt to exercise on crutches and walk with canes; or were pushed in wheelchairs by visiting relatives, or simply stood or leaned against poles and rails, to receive good wishes or chat with visitors. The internal corridors gave access to the rooms. In the lawns, were fixed benches on which patients sat and chatted with their visitors.

The two last rooms one of which Ndi occupied were a world of their own – designed to provide all the conditions and quiet (a door in the corridor shut out noise from the other rooms) necessary for recuperation. They were fantastically luxurious and expensive. For the three weeks that Ndi had been in hospital, the room opposite his was empty because of the price. And whenever the corridor door was shut, there was total quiet in his room. That of course had adverse effects on him. He needed company but very few people visited him and since he dreaded his third wife's company, he was virtually miserable. His only other visitor Mr. Ndeb, because of work imperatives, could only visit on Sunday evenings. Ndi was thus constantly left at the mercy of deep thoughts about his wealth, recovery, death and heir. The only way he could distract himself from the devastating thoughts was to indulge in eave dropping the conversations of adjacent rooms. Whenever a nurse shut the door of the corridor, he asked them to open it. On the fourth week of his admission into the hospital, the four patients whose conversations he eave dropped were discharged. For two days he remained alone in the hauntingly quiet ward.

On the third day, he heard some noise opposite his room. A nurse was having a heated confrontation with a lanky woman who seemed to be intruding into the Senior Service Ward. Ndi welcomed that human presence in the weird ward once more. He knew he would have the opportunity of eaves dropping conversations once more and thus get distracted from his worries. So, he paid keen attention to the exchange.

"Madam," the nurse addressed the woman. "I believe you have made a mistake in wanting to have your father admitted in this ward. This is the Senior Service Ward. This is the most luxurious and most expensive room in this hospital. Since I started work here two years ago, only two people have occupied it – the Secretary of State for Labour, and one Igbo tycoon."

"I have not made a mistake, major. This is the room I have paid for. Here is the receipt. I have just come down to see the state of the room before my father is brought here. He is in the intensive care unit for re-animation."

"Yes, I don't doubt your receipt. It is genuine but I am afraid you may be unable to pay the bills as time goes on. I have said this ward is not for every Dick and Harry. It is for people of very high calibre," the nurse said with a frown.

"Madam, what is your definition of senior service in relation to admitting patients into hospital wards? Is it bulk, beauty, work status, social status, political status, or the ability to pay? What yardstick have you used in judging my father's inability to occupy this room – my looks, since I know you have not yet seen my father? My bulk, since I know I am diminutive? Or my purse, since it is customary to hold that diminutive people are in the most part, poor, and thus can be brushed aside with the flick of the finger?" the woman asked disdainfully.

"Madam, don't take offence. I thought I was doing you a good turn. If I have made a mistake, forgive me. See the room then. I think it suits you. It is ready."

"Thank you for that apology. I am not taking offence for nothing. It is irritating to behold the audacity the bulky assume over the diminutive. I know you judge me from my size and awful looks. I am covered with dust. It's not my fault. It's the fault of our dusty roads. I travelled with my father all night on dusty roads. We had to arrive here this Friday morning in order to have him admitted before the week end. You see, I once worked in this hospital as a matron. But after the plebiscite that did not favour our joining Nigeria, I decided to return to the University Teaching Hospital Ibadan Nigeria, where I was trained and worked before coming to work in the Cameroons. I came home last week for holidays but met my father very sick. Although the Kumba hospital was nearer I decided to bring him here

27

where resuscitating conditions and lodging are better. There is no other honour I can give him than to have him admitted in a ward worth less than what I owe him. If there were a more expensive one, I would have preferred it. I am his only surviving child. We were four, two boys and two girls. All have died but me. My father is a senior service by any right. He can stake himself on me on the one hand, and on himself on the other hand. He is a no nonsense economic and social power house himself. And so, I, his rightful next of kin, owe him the honour to place him within our combined rights. It is the least I can do for him. If he died and there were a senior service mortuary, I would put his remains there. I am not blowing my trumpet. I am simply wanting to have things straight. And of course, I know, you know how we, diminutive fellows insist on our rights. So, please, promise me this favour, when they bring him, help me give him the treatment he deserves. I want to go to town to look for a hotel."

"I shall do, if they bring him before I hand over."

That conversation or exchange between the nurse and the woman played havoc on Ndi. He had thought it would distract him from his worries but it instead aggravated them. He took offence at the strong, authoritative, determined and unequivocal tone of the woman, made a tunnel view of her, and questioned who she was trying to impress. Was it he, he Ndi or some imaginary personality? Was she sent by some astral force to tell him indirectly that a woman had the audacity to choose and be given what she wanted? Why was she so pugnacious? If she were married, would she not have inflicted the same hurt on her husband as his third wife had inflicted on him? He deciphered the hand of queen Beelzebub in the speech of the woman, took a cane by his bed and violently pushed the door with it and shut it with a frightening bang. That was of course, not the best solution for him. As soon as he shut the door, he drifted into melancholy, into the full grip of uncanny thoughts.

Chapter Seven

Shortly after banging the door, two doctors and a throng of nurses brought the woman's father to the ward. They worked diligently to install all the lifesaving gargets they had brought along, and after ascertaining that every thing was in place, the matron now relaxed and satisfied, opened Ndi's door to find out how he was doing. Ndi was glad to see her. He knew her conviviality would distract him from his worries. But before either of them initiated a conversation, he peeped into the opposite room and saw the two doctors and nurses, and the sophisticated lifesaving gargets they were installing in the room. He took a deep breath as he juxtaposed the man's admission into the SSW with his and other patients'. It was like moving the intensive care unit for the sake of one man to the room. He considered that as an unethical fit of discrimination and wondered whether the hospital staff wanted every patient to be blessed with a matron in order to be given the same treatment. It was the first time that doctors accompanied nurses in the installation of a critically sick person in a room. More so, Ndi noticed that the doctors and the nurses spoke to the woman with a very high degree of respect. They addressed her matron Caro, and ended a response to her questions with a bow and a 'Yes or no, matron Caro'."

"Good morning and how are you today Mr. Ndi? Have you come to terms with yourself?" the matron started the conversation.

"Good morning matron. I feel a bit well. I am doing everything to come to terms with myself. It's not easy." he responded.

"Only a bit well? Everything will be alright. Don't worry. Get yourself together, forgive and forget, and you'll be OK."

"Matron, when will they remove this cumbersome waist cast?"

"When the doctor will ascertain that your discs have held on or are holding on. Once they remove the cast, they will remove the stitches and you will be OK."

"Who is the patient you have brought into the room opposite and what is wrong with him?"

"Matron Caro's father. He is suffering from several complications, including age. He is lucky that his daughter came on holiday just when he got into the crises. It has taken us hours of intense work to resuscitate him from the comatose state his daughter brought him."

"Matron Caro should be a very special person. You tend to adore her; all the intensive-care-unit staff came to escort her father."

"Matron Caro is of great renown. She was a matron in this hospital before independence. After the plebiscite, she went to work in Nigeria. We have great respect for her."

"It seems not everybody knows her. One of your nurses did not seem to know her."

"Yes, that should be one of the recently employed ones. Only the old nurses and doctors know her."

"She seems to be a very tough woman."

"For sure. She's astute, solid, knowledgeable and upright. We call her, 'The lady with the lamp'."

"I see. She's a male-lady then."

"She's more than that. Two men put together. I say, she is a no nonsense personality. You need see her on duty. Even doctors respect her. I raise my cap for her."

"Matron, when shall I start using the wheelchair? I am bored lying down in this room. For some days now, I have been alone in this building. Can you imagine how lonely it is? Agreed, there are always two nurses here but we don't have common ground for conversation. Furthermore, they come only when I call them for help. This is worse than a prison. If I could be wheeled around along the corridor my boredom would be manageable."

"That's the more reason why I say you should encourage your family to come to you. You are the least visited patient in this ward. Your friend Mr. Ndeb comes here very briefly only on Sunday evenings. He would have been the one to wheel you around. We cannot allow you at this point to strain in wheeling yourself up and down the corridors. You see, the corridors are not flat. They are made to slope to provide a strenuous up-wheeling task and a relaxing downward-roll on a wheelchair. This helps recovering patients to exercise and relax."

"It means, a tailless cow must only look onto God's mercy. Only God can drive away its flies."

"Mr. Ndi what do you mean? You mean you are tailless, tailless and in the SSW? You mean you will not forgive your wife and the rest of the people you believe have offended you?"

"I shall forgive them. I have even forgiven them but when a wound heals, doesn't it leave a scar behind? And when the beholder sees the scar what does he do, laugh?"

The matron felt a little growth of anger choke her. She rumbled the muscles of her irritated throat to ease up, and then she addressed Ndi, "Mr. Ndi. I thought we were friends but your hardheartedness is scaring me away from you. But while I expect that you will change, I shall assign one of the hospital hands on a little stipend to you, to do for you what a family member would have done more conveniently and freely."

"Thank you matron. I won't mind that."

"You won't mind that because you are not forgiving." the matron remarked sharply and left him unceremoniously with subdued anger.

31

After she had gone, Ndi realized his folly. He realized that his stone-heartedness had hurt her and she would probably withdraw from him. That would mean losing his main source of distraction. While he pondered on how to woo her back and reconcile with her, he heard her giving instructions to two nurses. She was instructing them on how to use the communications instruments to get in contact with the doctor on duty if the patient got into crises. She added that they should also put an ear on Ndi. Then she left.

Ndi was happy the matron still thought of him. While she was away, he cast back his mind on his evolution. The matron had made a sinister remark – "You are the least visited person in this ward". That remark tore through his bowels opening another gash of worries. Why was he the least visited patient? Why did his wealth not attract people to him? Was that too the design of queen Beelzebub? Was it because his daughters were not matrons? Was it because his wealth was not founded on sound solid education? Was it because it was not founded on sound family background? Was it because he related badly with both his former plantation-hand colleagues and superiors when he got into picking windfalls? As every passing second flooded him with torturing questions he thought of asking the matron to have him transferred to the common people's ward where the buzz and hums of patients and visitors would be a natural distraction. Unfortunately that day, Saturday, the matron avoided him. So he resigned himself to his fate.

On Sunday evening, he was astonished by the number of people who visited matron Caro's father. He doubted in whose honour the visitors came – that of her father or that of herself? It was not long however when he noticed that every visitor wanted matron Caro to take note of their presence in the crowd. So the massive visit was because of her and not her father. At first, the nurses allowed into the room, only two people at a time, then four, then six but when they realized that allowing in even eight people at a time won't make everybody see the patient within the time stipulated for visits, they put an end to the visit and advised matron Caro to move out and acknowledge the goodwill of the people. Immediately she stepped out, a forest of hands greeted her. After shaking hands with hundreds of people, she thanked them for the wonderful honour they had given her father on her behalf and said she was delighted that the people still had such wonderful memories of her.

Ndi did not take that showiness kindly. He condemned it as uncouth and unacceptable display of discriminatory popularity leading to preferential treatment of some patients. "A patient is a patient and all must be treated the same," he said in his heart and thought of confronting the matron for accommodating preferential treatment. And surely, he did during her late evening rounds.

"Matron, I believe if I were given the same attention as the patient opposite, I would have been standing and learning to walk by now."

"You think you are not given the same attention? That is vile talk. If the nurses hear it they will go in for punishing you by avoiding you. The patient you are talking about is sick, very sick. His condition fluctuates and so he needs attention and medicines by the minute to control his state. The medicines have to be administered by nurses. That is why you see nurses permanently by his side to administer treatment promptly if his condition deteriorates. You had an accident; you were operated, you need rest and strict discipline to recover. Do you want the nurses to assist you in resting and maintaining self-discipline? How feasible is that? I believe you have impaired judgment. If you won't mind, I would add that you are jealous of what you have failed to make of yourself. That patient is not to blame. He is not the crowd-puller, a devoted member of his family, his daughter is," the matron said firmly and left with a frown.

Chapter Eight

Ndi's hair stood on end as he pondered over what the matron had told him. He wondered whether her utterances were not tele-guided; that is, whether she was not under the influence of some weird forces. "Why should she have such a smooth, yet venom-squirting tongue? Whenever she starts a conversation, it entices one with its subtlety and civility; but towards the end, she makes a biting twist that stabs one right in the heart. For sure she is under the influence of queen Beelzebub. Does she know the meaning of, '…you are jealous of what you have failed to make of yourself'? Isn't that a stabbing provocation and reminder that I have failed to make great daughters out of my daughters? How great can a daughter be? The greatness of a daughter ends at crowd-pulling around a patient and that is all. What else? Furthermore, how could she have known about my debacle if she were not under the influence of queen Beelzebub? And she expects me to forgive a bitch that is responsible for my undoing? Never, never, never; if my recovery hinges on forgiving her, let me never recover," he said and curled in, waiting for an opportunity to pronounce the divorce of his first wife.

The opportunity came seven days later when Mr. Ndeb visited him. Ndi told him in straight terms to tell his first wife that he had divorced her and she should return to Bamenda – to her father's compound. He warned that if he recovered and saw her anywhere in the south, he would shoot and kill her. In spite of Mr. Ndeb's protest, Ndi was adamant. Mr. Ndeb returned and told the first wife that her husband had divorced her. She scrunched up a little, breathed in deeply and walked away pensively. Several strategies of return without raising alarm scuttled in her mind. In order to effect a hitch-free return, she feigned an emergency call from home. She told her co-wife, the third wife, that she had received a message from home that her stepfather had died and she would leave for Bamenda the next day. The third wife could not decipher any untoward moves in her speech or action when she saw her park everything she had. After all, if she were to be in Bamenda for a week, she needed all that she had in terms of dresses. She did not need the battered age-worn utensils in her kitchen. She knew taking her bed or any other cumbersome thing would trigger the raising of eyebrows and the asking of questions; and if her co-wife knew why she was returning to Bamenda, she would try to restrain her and perhaps call in other people. So she avoided all that was bulky. As such, there was nothing strange when she parked all that was necessary. The next day she left after bidding her co-wife good bye in the most cordial manner. It was after she had gone that the third wife discovered what had happened. She blamed Mr. Ndeb for not telling her about the divorce. She said if she had known about it she would have gone with the first wife.

On his part, Mr. Ndeb had expected the news of the divorce to crush the first wife and reduce her to a nose-running, heartbroken wretch that would scamper about soliciting intervention from Ndi's friends – he, himself being the primary. But he was dumbfounded and stunned by the readiness and contempt with which she accepted the divorce, and complemented it. Instead of displaying a tattooed mourning face and scuttling around counsellors begging them to intervene in a dispute she doubted the cause, a dispute that had cost her three teeth; she spited the divorce as if the marriage had been of no use to her. She did not only spite the divorce, she defied all that was associated with Ndi, including Mr. Ndeb.

Her reaction deflated Mr. Ndeb's ego. Shame-faced, he rushed to Victoria and told Ndi about the defiance.

"Massa, I did not know your first wife was that mulish. She is as stubborn as an untamed horse. When I told her about the divorce, she pouted, grimaced, entered her room and started parking. I have never seen such insolence. What might have led to that sort of spite? As I left the house, I thought she would reconsider her stand and run after me and tell me to intervene. She did not, nor did she send anybody to do so. The next day, her co-wife told me that she had left for Bamenda. I asked whether it was in response to the divorce. She started, and asked whether you had divorced her. I said yes. She yelled and said, 'then it would be twin divorce', that is, she would also go."

"Yes, I expected that from them. My first wife has to be insolent because I am in her palm. She knows what she has done to me. That bitch has ruined me. God punish her."

"I say even your third wife is behaving in a way not compatible with marriage ethics. I won't be surprised if I find that she has also gone."

"I know she too would want to divorce. It is a conspiracy. The two of them have conspired to undo me. Am I not her victim? Would she want to be with me again after reducing me to pulp? Am I sure of full recovery? Can I ever be a man again? See, it is for that bitch of a third wife that I am dying. She does not know the harm queen Beelzebub, my first wife has done to her. If she knew, she would kill her. That is how the world is. The people one thinks they love are the ones that kill them. My third wife has surprised me."

"Why do you call your first wife queen Beelzebub? It sounds so funny."

"I don't want to be worked up. I shall tell you my sad story when I return from this hospital. It is horrible."

Chapter Nine

Meanwhile, the matron and Ndi had been playing a cat and mouse game. For about a week, she skipped his room and only assigned nurses to talk to him and help him in case he needed help. That isolation unnerved Ndi. He had wanted a wheelchair and a hospital-hand to help push him around. He had agreed on putting the fellow a stipend. The only person who could provide that facility was the matron. Now she was avoiding him. One day, the day matron Caro's father was being discharged; he heard the matron gleefully chatting with the nurses who were helping in the discharge exercise. At some time, there was a lull in the conversation. Ndi made a desperate call to draw attention. The nurses and the matron rushed into his room to attend to him. Ndi feigned excruciating pains in the small of the back and groaned.

"What's wrong Mr. Ndi?" the matron asked with concern.

"My back is disintegrating. I feel agonizing pains in the small of my back because I am permanently lying on my back."

"Do you want to lie on your stomach? The nurses told me they make you lie halfway sideways these days. That is the normal progression. If you complain of sharp pains the doctor may want you X-rayed and if the discs are not holding, you may be subjected to another operation. I will bring him in tomorrow?"

"No, my problem is this misery, this isolation. Matron, you promised me a wheelchair. I am bored to the bone in this room. I hear my neighbour being discharged. My loneliness will now be more than doubled."

"Then say you want a wheelchair and don't pretend you have excruciating pains," the matron said half shouting. Then she called one of the male nurses and asked him to call Mula Kingue, one of the yard-boys, (cleaner) to bring a wheelchair. Presently, two nurses helped Ndi into the wheelchair and Mula started pushing him around the corridors of the SSW.

"This is the first time I have stepped out of this room in seven weeks. The seven weeks seem seven years. How beautiful it is to see the wide blue sky once more!" Ndi started a conversation.

"Seven weeks is small. Some people with back problems, especially those operated spend months lying on their backs. The matron has great respect for you. You might have worked magic on her. She hardly accepts that patients with waist casts be helped into wheelchairs. You are special, and I believe she has seen that you are progressing well. That is why she has allowed you onto a wheelchair," the boy remarked.

"How many times a week did you arrange with her to wheel me around?"

"She said I should ask you. It depends on you. I work from seven thirty in the morning to two o'clock in the afternoon. From then, I am free till seven in the evening. If you like me to wheel you around everyday, I shall do it."

"It is punishing remaining in the ward doing nothing, receiving no medicines and having nobody to talk to. I would like you to wheel me around everyday."

"OK, I shall do it from two thirty to six."

"That's OK for me. You know your stipend. You want an advance?"

"No, it would be more useful at the end of the month," the boy concluded, made a few more rounds and wheeled back Ndi to his ward.

Ndi was excited and thankful to the matron and Mula. That night he had a quiet smooth sleep. In the morning he got up fresh and hopeful, praying to have Mula wheel him around again that afternoon; and if possible as far as to the main road. As expected, Mula was punctual and very soon he was wheeling Ndi around.

"Any news?" Ndi started the conversation. "I just need any news. I am virtually empty and bored to the bone."

"There is no news apart from the stale news of the fight for inheritance. The patient in room 3 of your building was nearly killed two days ago by the children of Mr. Minyoli. Apart from that, there is no news."

"What happened?"

"It seems as if the Minyoli family is arguing that the man does not belong to their family and as such, has no right to inherit property in their family."

"If he does not belong to their family, how did he get there?"

"It is said Mr. Minyoli's late junior brother Mr. Lyonga had no issue with his wife. His wife had however, had a daughter Namondo with another man before she got married to him, and she had brought the child into the marriage with the approval of Mr. Lyonga. Because he had his marriage sanctified in church, he refused to marry another wife in spite of family pressure. Furthermore, he owed his elder brother a grudge because it was alleged that he had bewitched his wife and rendered her barren. That allegation caused a rift between the two brothers. While on his terminal sick bed, Mr. Lyonga invited a lawyer and bequeathed his property to his wife and her daughter who had, like her mother, begotten a child in Mr. Lyonga's house. By the time Mr. Lyonga died, nobody knew the worth of the property and there was no problem. But by the time his wife also fell terminally sick, the value of the property had begun unfolding itself. The hillock overlooking the

Centenary Stadium that nobody thought was worth a dime, started attracting Real Estate Developers who excavated gravel from it at 15, 000 Frs. a lorry load. The hillock was valued at millions of millions of francs of gravel. The gravel was said to be inexhaustible within the foreseen times. With that, the Minyoli family started showing interest in the property. Before the woman died, she, following her husband's instructions, bequeathed the property to her daughter and her son.

Now the Minyoli family has sued them arguing that Namondo and her son do not belong to their kin group and have no right to inherit property where they do not belong. With that, they want the court to abrogate the deed of inheritance and evict them from the place. The Minyoli family calls them intruding bastards.

On her part, Namondo brandishes the deed of the right to inherit. She argues that she is a foster daughter loved and recognized by the late man. As such she merits all the rights and prerogatives of a foster daughter including the right to inherit, and the right to transfer the right to her son," Mula explained.

"Do you think, Mula that if the child Namondo begot were a girl she would have had the guts to bequeath property to her? She did it because the child happens to be a boy," Ndi remarked.

"I don't think sex has anything to do with it. I think it is human folly. Both parties have already sold or pledged the property to second parties. Namondo, fearing that the Minyoli family could use uncanny means and seize the property from her sold it to a Bamileke man who has raised the price of a lorry load to 30, 000 Frs. The Minyoli family with a strong backing in the council has sold it to the council. While the Bamileke man is exploiting the western flanks, the council is exploiting the eastern. Both sides are pumping millions into the case," Mula said rather sadly.

"In the long run, neither of the belligerent parties would own the property. You see, Mula, a foreign culture has destroyed ours. How on earth can a man bequeath property to a barren woman and a string of bastards — the curse of his life? Can you imagine the untold problems a European culture has imposed on us? Because one is married in church he defies the obligation to procreate and insure the continuity of his lineage? And just think of it, the dog-licked-face woman was shamelessly audacious to bequeath the property to her bastard daughter. That your Mr. Lyonga was only good for early death, and thank God, he died early — stupid," Ndi insulted contemptuously and asked Mula to cut short the wheeling around and return to the ward.

"Mula was stunned with the degree of anger Ndi vented on a matter he thought did not concern him. "Should I come tomorrow? You look terribly upset with this first wheeling around."

"Yes, come tomorrow. I want to see the main road. If you wheel me to where women sell banana and assorted things, you can go. I shall wheel myself back since I shall only be descending."

Chapter Ten

The next day Mula came and wheeled Ndi to the main road where, under a huge tree women sold fruits and assorted things to a wide range of people – patients, visitors and even people from around the hospital quarter. The people took pleasure in coming to pass time under the tree and tell and listen to gossip around town. Ndi liked the shade for several reasons – it was cool, was the centre of attraction for convivial fellows from all walks of life, provided facilities for indoor games like draughts, and was a haven for mostly women petty traders and palm wine sellers and drinkers. So, it was ideal for him as a pastime and distraction from worries.

When he got to the tree, he met only a few people. That did not discourage him. He knew with a little patience others would come. And as sure as he had predicted he did not wait for long before the distraction came. A handicapped braggart Wase, came with a draughts board and challenged any bastard who would dare his skills in the game. Kalu, a master craftsman took the challenge and after betting the fellow and both of them giving the agreed sum to a referee, the game started. Wase took the first move with a tantalizing left flank trick. "Take that; your bastard of the first order," he shouted and slammed his hand (while taking the move) on the board shattering the discs out of their boxes. "Rough game, yellow card," the referee declared and cancelled the game with a warning for disqualification and forfeiture of money if Wase continued with disorder. "OK, I pity you," the fellow said with feigned courage. "I accept the

45

cancellation of the game," he said and told his opponent that the referee had saved him. Then he started the game anew. "Take that, your mami," he shouted again and made a gentler move. His challenger studied the positions of the discs and countered with a central manoeuvre that put his discs in a precarious position. Wase hissed as he saw the challenger fall into his snare; and moving his next disc rightward, cleared the board. "Bastard!" he insulted. The challenger surrendered and reshuffled the discs on the board to indicate the surrender. The referee declared Wase winner of the first game. But that was all he could win. His challenger had studied his left hand flank strategy and devised strategies to counter and puncture every move before it caused any damage in the subsequent ones. His strategy worked and he won decisively – 5 games to 1. As the braggart nursed the pain of his humiliating defeat, Ndi threw in a question.

"Gentlemen, your use of the word bastard is not compatible with civilized behaviour. All along, I have feared the insulted would take offence and become violent; but it seems as if, the word is one of the discs in your context. You make moves with it. What is your definition of the word? What does it mean?"

"Does it mean anything?" Wase asked. "Here, the word is used to disequilibrium the opponent and when he loses his bearings, he loses the game. That's all."

"You are joking. He loses his bearings because of the emotional impact of the word. That is what I want to find out. Who is a bastard?"

"A bastard is the product of illegal and unsanctified sexual relation between a man and a woman. In other words, a bastard is a child begotten out of traditional, civil or religious wedlock. Such a child belongs more to the mother than to the father. In most cases biological fathers don't even know of the existence of such children. Sometimes later in life they get embarrassed when such children are introduced to them or when an accident of history makes them discover the children. Though they may swear by the heavens about their innocence, they are betrayed by the undisputable resemblance that binds father and child. Then they sulk; and in guilt, apologize a million times for abandoning their blood in the wilderness at the mercy of hostile forces." the challenger chipped in.

"What then is the significance of the word bastard in your game?" Ndi asked.

"You see, the word is so commonly used here that nobody attaches any meaning to it. But if I should guess, the word might have originated here to imply that because bastards have no rights and prerogatives among their foster-fathers' kindred, they have no rights to play games meant for non-bastards. The only way bastards can claim such rights and prerogatives within this context is proving their worth in the game by winning," the challenger explained.

"That sounds interesting. Mr. Kalu, your name does not sound Cameroonian. Now that you have given your opponent, a Cameroonian, a resounding defeat, should I call it a crushing defeat? What next? Can he still call you a bastard?" Ndi asked.

"We here, do not call it a crushing defeat. We call it bastardization. He has been bastardized. For him to open his rotten mouth again, he has to de-bastardize himself by organizing at my convenience, a seven round tournament with me, and winning it. If he doesn't win, he remains a bastard. As you see, I have sealed his lips with wax. Look at him there – shame faced. Poor fellow. He has lost dignity and until he buys it back by winning the next tournament, nobody will allow him say a word amongst us."

"That sounds even more interesting – a bastard can be de-bastardized through a game metamorphosis. How wonderful that is!" Ndi exclaimed as a little growth of excitement made him burst into a guffaw.

The people around smarted glances at each other; surprised at Ndi's strange behaviour. They thought he was out of place. They had never seen him before. He was not part of them. Where did he come from and what was his mission? Why was he so excited among people he did not know? Concluding therefore that Ndi was a pugnacious unwelcomed intruder, they in one accord, as if they had conspired to boycott contact with him brushed him aside. Ndi deciphered some suppressed hostility and disapproval in their countenance and made good his state by promising to sponsor either the seven round tournament the next day if both parties agreed, or sponsor seven rounds of palm wine drinking to the people. That offer softened hard hearts and paved the way for his integration into the under-tree community. It was a fantastic experience – an experience that had launched him into an entirely new world. He had enjoyed the distraction and the camaraderie he had created and looked forward to being the main attraction the next day when all attention would be directed to him. He was full of joy and as he prepared to return to the ward, Mula came, and wheeled him back.

"How have you enjoyed your evening, Sir?" Mula asked.

"Fantastic. I have never seen a welcoming group like the one I met under the tree. They are wonderful in everything. They are creative, sharp and witty. You can't get bored among them. They calm down tempers of the aggrieved and give hope to the depressed. I had a gleeful time," Ndi responded.

"Congratulations. Will you want to be wheeled there again tomorrow, Sir?"

"Yes, of course, if that won't annoy the matron."

"It won't. All she is interested in is that you relax ideally."

"OK, come again tomorrow. Same time."

Chapter Eleven

Ndi had never had a quiet and smooth night like the one he had after his first encounter with the under-tree community. For the first time since he met Fai Nchotu and was told about his first wife's double nature, and her role in his undoing, he had never had a straight six hour sleep. He had never been distracted to the point forgetting about his wealth, his worries about his next of kin and the fate of his first wife. When he got up in the morning, he felt as if he had sloughed a cancerous skin. He was a new man. Time and again, the terms, bastardization and de-bastardization came into his mind and made him purse his lips trying to suppress outbursts of laughter. He took pleasure in the words for no apparent reason. Whenever they popped up in his mind, he sniggered, shrugged his shoulders and took very deep breath. He doubted whether it was not the logic of de-bastardization that made Mr. Lyonga to indirectly bequeath his property to his barren wife's grandson.

As these things occupied his mind, time passed fast. He was surprised when Mula knocked at the door to announce that it was 2.30 pm and therefore time for another under-tree adventure. He prepared fast and Mula wheeled him to the tree and left him there to have his fun. Ndi had thought he would meet an enthusiastic community waiting for him and give him a resounding welcome. But when he got to the place he saw only four palm wine-selling women arranging sitting positions, and palm wine cups on makeshift tables. He noticed that they had brought four times more cups than the previous day perhaps because they were expecting a heavy drink-for-free turnout. Word had gone round that a wealthy patient would flood the under-tree community with palm wine.

After the women had arranged the place, they sat down to wait. Ndi had no choice but to wait with them and listen to their conversation.

"My sister," the eldest woman addressed the woman near her. "I hear when matron Caro brought her father here, the whole Victoria came out to pay their respects to him. I was not here. I went to Douala to see my son."

"Mamiyo! I was there myself. I tell you, I have never seen such a crowd before. Some women are more than men. Even doctors adored matron Caro. Her father was treated like a king," the lady responded.

"You see, there are children and there is a child. A person may have children but lack a child. It is better for God to give a person a child than children. To me, a child is a child – boy or girl. See, when chief Mutombi, the chief of Victoria was sick and was brought to this very hospital who knew he was sick? Yet he had a compound full of boys each praying that he should die for them to inherit property. And when he finally died, the fellows were shamelessly at daggers-drawn. But see what honour matron Caro has brought upon her father!"

"That is not all," interjected the youngest of the women. "Sister Caro has taken her father to Europe for further treatment. As they left here, they went straight to Nigeria and from there to Europe. Sister Caro's first son, a medical doctor is married to my younger sister. I am very close to the family."

"Matron Caro has a son? When did she have him?" the eldest woman asked.

"You think all women are stupid? When she found that she was not blessed with marriage, she decided to have her children. She has four children, three boys and one girl. Her children are the pride of her father. And you know what?

Very intelligent children. One of the boys is a chartered accountant, and the other is a business man in Nigeria. That is the one who is planning to come back home and manage his grandfather's cocoa plantations. You see that new story building at Mukeba road junction, he is building it. The girl is still studying in the University of Ibadan. She begot the children in Nigeria and educated them there. Her father knew she was having children in Nigeria but he never told anybody in the village. So, the day sister brought the children to the village and showed them to her paternal family, her father's brothers who had thought they would inherit his property because they thought he had no male heir, were flabbergasted. Sister Caro is tough."

"Matron Caro is really, 'small no be sick', (being diminutive is not being sick). Tell me; is that how she has killed elephants? Thank God. What else does a woman want on earth? God never forgets good people."

Two people came in noisily just as the last speaker was ending her response.

"Please, please keep quiet, we are conversing. Please," Ndi supplicated with them.

"Ah! What conversation are you having with women?" one of the men reacted contemptuously.

"A conversation about matron Caro," Ndi responded.

"What has matron Caro done that no other person cannot do?" the man asked with spite.

"Please, if people are to ask that question, it is not people like you. The other day I met you dying of malaria, common malaria. You hadn't a single aspirin. I forced you to go to hospital at my own expense. Am I lying? Sister Caro brought her father to this hospital and the world shook. She put him in the most expensive ward and the world admired. After the treatment here, she flew him to Europe and the world is gasping. What else did you want her to do that you cannot do? The only thing you can do which she cannot do is beg for a cup of palm wine," the youngest of the women blasted.

51

"Enanga, be careful; very careful with your venom squirting tongue. If you play, I can send you sprawling in hospital with a backhand slap. Idiot. You are talking of a bitch that will make Nigerians inherit her father's property as if having a string of bastards merits wining a medal? Should we go singing the national anthem because she has achieved in promiscuity what she could not in politics? Those are fools who wanted us to join Nigeria," the fellow retorted.

"How many bastards have you? Can you father a bastard? How old are you? Are you married? You want to be a full stop in your lineage and you are not even ashamed of yourself. Whether her children are bastards or not, they are worthy bastards; not *hurohuro wahala* – empty sacks that can't stand on their own. Sister Caro's bastards are rain that defies umbrellas, the pumpkin that knows no boundaries, and the sky that has no limits. They are the Perl every mother would want to have, not running-nosed big-mouthed vases scuttling for drink-for-free, bee laden palm wine," Enanga responded in the manner of a village quarreller.

"If palm wine is that useless, why are you selling it? You bite the finger that feeds you. Can you live without selling palm wine? Stupid," the fellow insulted.

"Please, I don't want us to spoil the evening. We have come here to pass time, to recreate and make friends and to exchange ideas. So calm down and let's make the evening worthwhile. Madam, serve yourself a cup and serve the gentleman a cup, drink and exchange cups and deflate your tempers." Ndi supplicated. The woman hesitated but after the intervention of the eldest, she did as Ndi had said and the two belligerent calmed down.

Chapter Twelve

Madams," Ndi addressed the women. "I need not be buying the wine in cups. I better buy all the jugs and ask you to help serve the guests as they come in. But I am afraid the wine is not much. You have only four jugs and I believe the turnout would be heavy. How much is that?"

"Sixteen thousand francs – four thousands a jug. More wine will come. By the time we finish this, the tapers will bring evening wine. But if we do as you say, we shall not be here for ten minutes. I know my people when it concerns drink-for-free. So, if the people come, handover the entertainment to me," the youngest of the women, Enanga, suggested. And immediately the people came, Ndi introduced her as the MC of the occasion.

In taking control, she thanked him for the honour he had given her in making her the MC of the occasion. Then she addressed the people.

"Under-the-tree people, please, I think we should be thankful to the host of honour for his generosity. I would call this a windfall day. It is hard these days to see such magnanimity. If he can be so generous in the wheelchair, then he is wonderful when he is in good health. But we should not abuse his generosity. He is buying the first two rounds for each and every one of us, and after that, those who will still want to continue drinking, and I know there would be many, would have to dip their hands into their pockets. You don't ride a willing horse to death. So, the first round, the thirsty people's round and the second round, the gentlemen's round are free. The third round, the greedy people's cup, and the fourth round, the drunkards' cup, and the fifth round, the gutter people's cup are paid for by the drinker. I call then on my fellow women to serve the thirsty people's cup. We all know the speed with which it is drunk."

The women served the thirsty people's cup and within a second, the drinkers stretched forth their cups, asking for the gentlemen's cup – the cup of restraint drinking. The women served the gentlemen's cup. The people sipped a bit of the wine and knowing the consequences of emptying the cup fast, held the virtually full cups in their hands as one holds a baby about to sleep. Some put their cups on the makeshift tables to avoid the temptation of sipping more frequently. That controlled drinking, of course, led to conversation. And as the saying goes, 'he who pays the piper determines the tune', Ndi let the conversation.

"Ladies and gentlemen, when a person loses a game of draughts amongst you, he undergoes degradation known in your jargon as bastardization. For him to regain uplifting he must win. You call that uplifting, de-bastardization. Now, when a woman does what only a man is expected to do, she definitely undergoes uplifting. What do you call that uplifting, manification or malification? In fact I want us to coin a name for matron Caro's prowess. The floor is open."

"A woman can do only some and not all the things a man can do. So, she remains always a woman. For example, she cannot piss in a bottle. So whatever matron Caro does, remains within the circle of her woman-ness," Mr. Ntola chipped in.

"This world has changed. A woman was not expected to do what men did. In the days of old, the woman was expected to nurse children and take care of the household. Today, we say, what a man can do a woman can do. That is upsetting the world. I know also that what a woman can do, a man cannot do. A man cannot conceive, a man cannot suckle children and that is it," Mr. Eyalle said.

"There is nothing like manification or malification in the same way as there is nothing like womanisation or feminisation. Only the squint eye sees a woman's prowess as uplifting. Uplifting from what to what? I think what there is, is naturization. By this I mean, respecting what nature is all about. Matron Caro has neither looked low nor high on her nature or any other nature. She has never despised men. She has never also elevated them. She relates with them as a woman should and carries out her duties as a woman should. She is a strong advocate of breastfeeding. She told us, she breastfed all her children. You know what breastfeeding does to a woman and how some women shun it. She did not shun it because she considered it her nature, and that of course makes her an ideal woman. In relation to what we call her prowess, all she did was to improve on her feminine nature and emerge as an icon worthy of emulation. If we want to honour her, it should not be because she is a male-woman but because she is a super-woman – a woman that knows what a woman's nature is, improves on it and uses it appropriately," Enanga expounded.

"I buy Enanga's views. Her views are that the base problem is management of resources, skills and nature, if not nature, skills and resources. Men have always misunderstood and distorted the design of nature. They have even gone as far as changing the design of the bible. In the bible it is clearly stated in Mark 10:7 - 8, "And for this reason a man will leave his father and mother and unite with his wife, and the two will become one, so they are no longer two, but one." A man will leave his father and mother's homestead for his wife's homestead and the two will unite. That is the design of the bible. But in their greed and usurpation men in interpreting this, have hijacked the supreme position of the woman in marriage. Instead of the man leaving his homestead, he makes the woman leave hers and so degrades her into a stranger and makes her occupy an inferior position in the union," Mamiyo said with anger forming a lump in her throat and making her voice coarse.

"You are perfectly right, Mamiyo. Men look at things with the squint eye. See, when two men own two stables; stable one, of female goats only; and stable two, of he-goats only, the man with the stable of female goats only, does not say the offspring belong to the man with the stable of he-goats only. In other words, he recognizes that possession in the animal world is not male-based, but female-based. This is the natural way things work. But men in their greed and usurpation turn things upside down. In the world of human beings, possession is male-based. Have a boy and a girl. All sex offenses of the boy are frowned at with silver linings but those of the girl are frowned at with scourging scorn. In other words, deep down in the hearts of both parents, the boy is a hero and is encouraged, while the girl is a debased harlot and is derided. The boy's illegal children are held in high esteem than those of the girl," Enanga stormed in with a trembling voice.

"You are delving into a complex issue of how men should relate with women. The bible does not give the woman the prerogatives you claim it gives her. At the time of creation, if I should also refer to the bible, God created man out of the earth and blew His breath, the breath of life, into him. So man is the direct product of the earth – the earth was made for man. But when he became lonely, God decided to create for him a helper. To avoid creating for him a helper that would be a rival, he did not form the helper out of the earth. He formed the helper out of part of the man. He chose a part that would neither make the helper too inferior nor too superior. So, he neither chose the part from his foot, nor from his head. He chose a part midway and formed woman. Woman means, midway. That midway choice is the determining factor of the relationship between man and woman. The man cannot therefore move compound in marriage, the woman should. As to what concerns stables of she-goats and he-goats, the problem is simple. The she-goat carries home the offspring; the he-goat does not carry home the offspring. So, the offspring belongs to the home to which it is carried to. In the human world, if a he-man wants to carry home the offspring, he must sanctify the union with bride price, that is, he must own the she-man. In like manner, if the owner of the he-goat stable wants the offspring, he must own the she-goat."

"Ladies and gentlemen, we must go beyond the gentlemen's round. I now offer unlimited rounds especially as evening wine has begun coming in. So, don't shy in having your capacity rounds," an elated Ndi interjected. "Empty your cups and let's cheer ourselves up. I believe we have an interesting topic before us. The women are out-speaking the men. We need reaction from the men." Saying that, he stretched out his cup for the women to refill it with the less alcoholic sweet evening wine and encouraged the frugal men to empty their cups and do the same. The men emptied their cups and asked for the third helping also. As they drank, they pondered over the women's onslaught.

"Let me also react to what Enanga has said," Mr. Zacs stepped in. "Most people who have only daughters nowadays make them inherit their property. The introduction of Letters of Administration and the legalization of certificates of next of kin have neutralized the male-based traditional inheritance. More so, education tends to play havoc on girls. People tend not to like marrying educated girls for two main reasons; the first being the high degree of barrenness amongst them and the second being their uppishness. So with that, things are changing,"

"You have got it wrong, totally wrong again. How many educated girls do you see around? For every one educated girl, there are a thousand educated boys because fathers readily send the boys to school and the girls to marriage. I am an example. No boy ever beat me in class. But my father sent my brothers to Sasse and sent me to marriage – thus indirectly to palm wine selling. You talk of educated girls being barren. That is not true. All educated girls I know, who got married have children. Madam Esu, a Ghanaian was well past the age before the money mongering Esu married her. Mr. Esu was marrying money not children. That lone case cannot call for generalization. That is where sister Caro beats other women. She took a quick decision and made good use of it. Once she saw age threats, she decided to have her children. She knew she could bring them up without the assistance of a husband – husband my foot. When her father was educating her, there was that bullshit talk of his wasting his money on another person's property. Is she somebody else's property today? In her father's village, is there a single man who sent only his sons to school, who can loosen the lace of his shoes today? Do you think if sister were married she would have abandoned her father to death because she belonged to somebody else?" Enanga asked in self-pity anger.

"Enanga, you need not blow your top. I think the problem is that, marriage makes the girl move compound. I need not mince words on this. There is something beyond human understanding that compels a girl to prefer marriage to being single with the intent of recovering and possessing her father's threatened homestead. Ninety percent of the girls look forward to the day they would marry. It is not the question of misinterpreting the bible. It is a fact. And a father, who finds himself surrounded by girls, sees the fate of his homestead with disquiet. In the same vein, there is something beyond human understanding that compels boys to take the defence of their fathers' homestead as their primary task. As such, they shun moving compounds no matter the circumstance. A boy who moves compound is branded a he-goat, a worker without pay, because he cannot claim the offspring of the union," Mr. Esoka explained.

Ndi made a quick review of Mr. Esoka's intervention and found that it hit the epicentre of his stand on the issue of having only daughters. Daughters move compounds when they get married. That likelihood of moving compound is the bedrock on which their rights and prerogatives in their paternal homesteads are determined. Since it is more likely that a girl-child would move compound if she gets married, than to doubt whether she would marry or not, tradition gives precedence to moving compound; and so, right at birth considers her married, and thus a temporary entity in her paternal homestead. A temporary entity cannot be given the rights and prerogatives of next of kin. In case of daughters only, who steps in? For sure, daughters only put the homestead in jeopardy.

Furthermore, even in a situation in which a given daughter doesn't get married and decides to keep her father's compound, her hold on the compound is determined by the man she keeps. In most cases, the man, knowing his sojourn is provisional, turns out to be an exploiter or a downright thief. If he decides to marry the girl, and the two keep the homestead, he counterpoises his moving compound with imposing and making his genealogy primary. That of course, upsets the protocol of the two kin groups in the homestead and generates a breach of harmony among the living and the dead. The dead claimants of prime of place (the lady's aggrieved paternal ancestors) take revenge on the couple by inflicting misfortunes on them. The living claimants of prime of place (the lady's paternal uncles and cousins) spite the couple and show overt hostility whenever the couple tries to protest against inevitable discrimination. The claimants readily tell them to return to where they belong, that is, the man's homestead. If that is said in the presence of his children, and of course, most of the time it is said in their presence for greater effect, the children sulk in shame and lose self-confidence. That plays havoc on their psychic and they shy in taking authority in matters concerning the homestead. Thus, neither the fellow nor his children are accepted; and that seriously destroys the raison d'être of a homestead. And so, regrettably so, sons by daughters are not good enough to be one's next of kin. "They are not, not i, i, ideal," Ndi stammered in his heart, lamenting his situation.

While Ndi was pondering over Mr. Esoka's intervention, wine was getting the better of the people and they were at each other's throat – quarrelling over irrelevant things and extending insults to family members who were not there. Enanga reacted promptly. She closed the occasion by withdrawing all the cups and stopping the serving of more wine. "You see, that is why I call you animals. You are abusing generosity. What impression do you want to give the host of honour? Do you want to show him that drinking for free stupefies you? I am scandalized by your behaviour. Furthermore you insult people who are not here. That is stabbing in the back. That is not correct. With your permission, I make a fervent apology to him on your behalf and promise him a better organization next time. I now call on him to say something if he has a word for those of us who are still sober," she concluded and handed the floor to Ndi.

Ndi started and lost tract of what to say. After a series of e, e, e, e, he thanked the people for giving him the honour he thought he did not deserve among them and promised more evenings like that in future. He prayed that God should safely take them home as he had brought them safely. And with that, Mula, who had come on time, wheeled him to the ward.

Ndi was visibly shaken by the implications of the facts he deciphered from the discussion. Every passing minute unfolded new insight into Mr. Esoka's intervention. Ndi intermittently shook his head as Mula wheeled him to the room. Gall oozed into his mouth; he spat out what he could and swallowed what he could not. He concluded that, the only option left for a man with daughters only is to keep looking for a son. A son is the only insurance for the preservation and maintenance of the homestead – a sanctuary whose raison d'être is the per-foliation of people (the living and dead) of the same paternal blood. That would have been easy if nature worked in the way man desired. But it does not. Nature does not work to satisfy the whims and caprices of man. So, even in the question or preserving and maintaining paternal genes, nature works contrary to the desired principle. Several unimaginable and disheartening things come into play, that is, various types of sons via for position in a situation that only one type is most acceptable. In reality what types of sons vie for that sanctuary – the homestead? That question raised Ndi's pulse instantly as four types of sons whirled in his mind's eyes; especially as he found himself encaged in the most undesired one. First, is one's 100% blood sons (the most preferred) second, sons by inheritance or adoption (late relatives' sons, the ones tradition expects one to guide to maturity and allow to survive and revive their fathers' homesteads or found theirs) third, sons by marriage (the ones unfaithful wives impose on husbands) and fourth, sons by unmarried daughters?

Ndi juxtaposed the two last types with a disquieting analysis: sons by marriage were worse than sons by unmarried daughters. Whereas it was crystal clear that sons by unmarried daughters carried their grandfather's genes, sons by marriage carried no such genes. They were completely strange blood. Their presence in a homestead therefore defied the homestead. They had blood relations only with their mothers and not with their purported fathers. They were as such, out of the question, in other words, not sons at all in a patrimonial system.

Yet, because some old folks with daughters only, consider them as 'half a loaf is better than no bread', and console and stake themselves on them, and secondly because of the intrigues of their mothers, sons by marriage tend to be more favoured and made to whirl powers and have more prerogatives in their foster fathers' homestead than the sons of unmarried daughters in the same homestead. Sons of unmarried daughters are readily called bastards but nobody dares call marital sons bastards. "Why this?" Ndi asked himself. He trembled and shook his head as a distressing ready answer dashed into his brains. "It is because the mothers of sons by marriage shroud their relation with their husbands with a smokescreen – a decoy that presents the husbands as the veritable fathers of the sons. And of course, the outflanked ignorant husbands succumb to the lies and chest-pound themselves as the fathers of the fakes. With that, society follows suit in recognizing the decoy as the real thing and gives honour where it is not due."

Ndi wilted instantly as that answer slashed through him. He sighed and shook his head and concluded that, no matter from what angle one looked at it, the acquisition of a veritable next of kin was fraught with intrigues – intrigues which were becoming more and more insurmountable because unfaithful wives were becoming more sophisticated in designing decoys. In the same vein, it was difficult to stake one's homestead on unmarried daughters' sons. Neither the unmarried daughters, nor their offspring were of use to a person longing for a genuine next of kin. He, Ndi, as father of six unmarried daughters had to look for a son who would be his next of kin. And this, he would tell the matron when next she visited him. He would be frank to tell her that he would not forgive even his third wife who was responsible for the pain he was suffering from. Once he got well he would marry a virgin – one of the daughters of a plantation-hand who would fall prey to his wealth, and God willing, they would be blessed with a son. After all, the seer, Fai Nchotu had predicted it. Convinced he was on the right track, he waited for Mr. Ndeb to visit him. And once he did, he told him to tell his third wife that she was persona non grata.

Chapter Thirteen

Ndi had a throbbing headache as he got into his room. What he had thought would be a relaxing pastime, turned out to be very strenuous. He had over-tasked his brains in analyzing the intervention of Mr. Esoka and that had given him a headache. He took two aspirin tablets and tried to wait for them to calm his nerves before lying down to sleep. That deliberate interference with the forces of sleep did him some good as he realized that he could not resist. He lay down and very soon snored away.

In the morning, the matron stopped by during her rounds to chat with him. She found him rather tense and withdrawn.

"Mr. Ndi, you seem not to be yourself today. Any problem? Any more pains?" she asked.

"Good morning matron. I feel fine though clouded with problems. I am, should I say, a cursed man. I have too many problems, matron. I have decided to divorce my third wife. She caused me this accident. She has contributed to my problems."

"Mr. Ndi, can you tell me a person who has no problems? I know, as a rich man you have problems. All rich people have problems. It may be your long stay in the hospital is costing you your businesses. But that is human nature. So long as you are here, try to forget your problems. Focus on your recovery. And once you are well you will regain your businesses. I have told you to reconcile with your family rather than divorcing."

"My businesses are well managed. I have very competent white managers. Everything is going on well. But there is one thing I lack, and that is my worry. I lack a next of kin. I have not got a son to inherit my property when I die. I have seven daughters. The eldest is married. The others are there dragging big breasts all over the place."

"What scorn! What vile talk! What rotten inside! They are girls, and therefore they must have breasts. What did you want them to have? You disdain and deride your daughters because they are not boys?" the matron snapped.

Ndi shrank in shame and apologized. "Matron, you see, our culture looks low on any rich man who has no sons. That is what is making me bitter. We consider a man with viable sons richer than a man with material wealth. I have material wealth, I believe you can't count five people in this country without me, but I have no son. So, traditionally, I am no good. If I die, who will lead the dignitaries of our community to the celebrations of my death? I am sorry, but. I don't mean harm to my daughters."

"You definitely do. You mean harm to your daughters and that is why I don't see them here. They hardly come to visit you. But see, the patient who was opposite you has only one daughter. You have seven. His daughter makes him proud. Your daughters make you depressed. It means your value scales are not functioning well. If a person with one daughter is happy, and a person with seven is not, then of course, if the person with seven were given one daughter, his sorrows would be double because he would be aspiring for more. Of course I know you are basing your argument on the philosophy of some primitive tribes in Cameroon that say a woman is worth nothing. But don't forget, it is the woman who begets the boys who are worth the world."

"Matron, please, I don't think we have to say it with drawn brows. We both know where the shoe pinches. If I could swallow the bitter pill I would readily do so. But there is no way I can bury the truth."

"Mr. Ndi, you are a dormant volcano. Your inside is black, worse than sin because you are working on fixed orders. There are no fixed orders in the world. You believe boys propagate fixed orders better than girls. That is false. Inasmuch as there are no fixed orders, there are situations in which girls have performed better in managing the transient orders that are our potions on earth."

"Matron, what do you mean by transient order? Is one's homestead – a sanctuary of the living and the dead, a transient order?"

"Have you never heard of an extinct kin group? If not, look around Victoria, look around Mankon, and look around Douala. See how once very prominent families are faring. Where are the Pharaohs of Egypt? Who are their heirs? Go round the world and you will see thousands of cases like that. For every yesterday, there is a today, and for every today, there is a tomorrow. A yesterday, a today and a tomorrow need not be separated by twenty four hour intervals, they may be separated by whatever number of hours are ideal for the supreme owner of orders."

"That's becoming too sophisticated."

"Sophisticated and true," the matron said disdainfully and left.

Chapter Fourteen

Ndi felt relieved when the matron left. The whole day lay before him – an unpredictable day. He doubted whether his encounter with the matron was not the prelude of things to come that day. He thought of the under-tree community. He admired Enanga. If only he could chat with her. But suppose she too turned waspish, how would he end the day?

Mula came as usual on time and wheeled him to the under-tree. Only Enanga and one other woman were there. Customers had not begun coming. Ndi thought that was the best time to start a conversation with her.

"Madam Enanga, Good afternoon. How are you today?"

"As the men want me to be."

"How can they determine how you should be, are they God?"

"They are more than God."

"What makes you say that? You have a problem with Ogah?"

"Who is Ogah?"

"Your husband."

"If he is my Ogah, who am I to him"

"His wife."

"Only that, mere wife? OK, is it only when I have a problem with my husband that there is a problem? There is a problem, an eternal problem not only with me and my husband but with all women and men because when God created man, He asked him to create woman to be his helper. Man, unused to creating, created an imperfect thing and named it woeman. And when woeman protested against the negative connotations of its name he put an alloy to it and called it, woman."

"What chapter and verse are you quoting? I hope I have not bumped into a sad situation?"

"I am quoting the under-tree bible, chapter cup of drunkards, verse tall talk."

Enanga's joke-twist brightened up Ndi. He had thought she had a problem at home which he had unintentionally rekindled. But with the twist, he realized she was just exhibiting palm-wine-selling wit. Yes, sellers and consumers of alcohol have double natures – the normal or low, and the abnormal or high. When exposed to the influence of alcohol indirectly (like the sellers) or directly (like the drinkers), they time and again transcend the normal and dwell in the higher realm, a realm of 'speaking in tongues'. And the more they stay in either of the two influences, the more their two natures merge; as elements of the high gradually permeate those of the low, making the two indistinguishable in the end.

"Your bible is unwritten, that is why I could not remember the chapter and verse. Good, your customers have not begun coming."

"They know when to come. They come when the wine has seasoned. Only those who drink less alcoholic wine come early. Those who drink real wine, wine that has aged with time come later."

"So where do you put me?"

"You are sick. Yesterday, you drank with restraint. So, one cannot judge you from your wheelchair."

"Madam Enanga, you are fantastic. I admire you. I was so impressed with the way you handled the people of the under-tree yesterday."

"Thank you for the compliment. I also admired the way you took the abuse. Do you remember that after that generosity, the drunks had no curtsey to thank you? I think it is the nature of men in general. I say so because it occurs time and again. Men are ungrateful."

"Do you think women are better?"

"I think so. I have never seen a situation in which women have exhibited the degree of ungratefulness that men exhibit. Or, it may be perhaps, because women are not prone to drinking. It is here, this under-tree, that men massacre their wives and girlfriends. Once they get high, they unethically drain their entrails about the goings on with their partners; each claiming to hit the core of the truth about women. Even crowned dunces claim to be philosophers. Horrible, men are horrible."

"I think the equation is balanced because if one were to go to a place of convergence for women he would hear them do the same on men."

"No, women have less time and space for men. They make very little claims on them."

"Do you think the world would have been better if it were possessed by woman alone?"

"If it weren't better when it was possessed by man alone, it wouldn't be better if it were possessed by woman alone."

"Where does this lead us to then?"

"It's simple; it leads us to complementarily. One can't do without the other. And that's it."

"But one is pivotal, the centre of being; the other is peripheral."

"Bullshit. There's nothing like that. In counting two we begin with one. But we don't stop at one, we get to two to complete."

"You heard what Mr. Esoka said yesterday about the midway-ness of the woman. I thought he made a point."

"He had a right to express his impish and limping logic. It was a way of justifying the existing system of comprehensive male supremacy. I am not an advocate of that. I am an advocate of individual male or female success story. Look, here where I am, I am the door of this society – I see in and out. I know every bit of thing about everybody in this town and even in Buea. Cars mean nothing to me. Suits mean nothing to me. I sell palm wine but I lend money to car owners. See, it was here that the outcome of the plebiscite was decided. So, people like Esoka who hide behind the smokescreen of comprehensive male supremacy should be allowed to have their daily bread by it. "

"That's the doctrine of, 'what a man can do, a woman can do', right?"

"If not better," the other woman interjected. "Some women do better in some cases. I shall give you an example. My late uncle, Pa Bisong of Manyemin had eleven children with his two wives – ten boys and one girl. Unfortunately he lost his first wife in Enugu Nigeria soon after he settled there. About three years later, his second wife died when she came home to bury her mother at Etuka village. She suffered from dysentery and died. Pa remained a widower for about five years when he came home to bury his elder brother who was chief. After the burial, he was persuaded by the population to takeover the vacant chieftaincy stool because his elder brother left no male heir. Pa was chief for only two years when he fell terminally ill. When his lone daughter heard of the illness, she abandoned her interests in Nigeria and came to assist him. You know chieftaincy in Buea Province – the chief fends for himself. So the girl had to fend for her father and herself. She recuperated all the farms that her uncles had seized from her father's labourers when he was away, and before long, they had enough to carry them on. But can you imagine that when Pa was dying he bequeathed all his property to his sons – sons who did not care whether he was sick or not? His daughter got wild and backed by the villagers, made Letters of Administration in her name. Her brothers are still to acknowledge that their father is dead. Today, go to Manyemin and see how prosperous that girl is. She is the backbone of the royal family because her male nephews and cousins are as useless as her brothers."

"That's a very beautiful story. What about the chieftaincy stool, is she the chief now? And what will happen to the property and the stool when she dies?"

"One of the husks is the regent chief but in fact, she is the force behind the chief. As for the property, she has two children one girl and one boy."

"There's no doubt that some men are husks. But e, e, e, e, furthermore, we look at things differently. In Bamenda Province, there is no gainsaying when it concerns next of kin. Girls don't inherit. But down south here, tradition is much looser."

"So, in Bamenda, what does a man with only daughters do? Bequeath his property to his brothers? And what happens to the daughters if they are not married?" Enanga asked.

"Daughters don't stay unmarried in Bamenda or in any polygamous system. Polygamy solves the problems of widowhood and single-womanhood. But those who, in spite of this, choose to stay unmarried fend for themselves in townships. Unmarried girls are unheard of in villages."

"You call that slavery marriage? That is not marriage. Are you from Bamenda?"

"Yes, I am. I come from Bamenda, though I have spent most of my life in Tiko."

"So you have many wives then. How many, twenty or forty?"

"I have been married to three, though at the moment I am married to none."

"You divorced them? What happened with you?"

"The evil hand of fate played havoc on us. I have, as you say, divorced my wives, my first wife and my third. My second wife died in childbirth. If I recover from this wheelchair, I will have to marry again for one thing, I don't have a next of kin with any of my wives. I have seven daughters but no son."

"You have seven daughters but no next of kin? What do you mean by next of kin? Does next of kin to you mean a boy? Furthermore, at your age do you think you can make children again? Even if you can, don't you think they will be hornbill-headed children – sick-prone-things with running noses, always last in class, causing incessant problems to caring mothers?" Enanga asked with steaming anger.

"Why can't I father children? Older people do. I don't see any reason why I cannot."

"Yes, but suppose you do not? I am asking this because of several reasons and several solutions."

"What are the reasons?"

"One, suppose your accident cost you your manhood? Two, suppose girls down south refuse marrying you?"

"First, there are traditional doctors. Second, I shall forage for a wife from among the rustics of Bamenda in Tiko, Mutengene, Victoria and Buea. Most, if not all plantation-hands are from Bamenda."

"That will be hunting snakes. You want to lure innocent girls into a wealth snare. Wealth is like wet carbide. It can ignite a girl beyond expectation no matter her origins."

"What are the solutions?"

"The first is, adopting a male heir if you think it is only male heirs you want. Go to the orphanage and choose a boy you like. Or choose your immediate paternal family boy. The second solution is surrendering yourself to the current of fate and allowing it wash you ashore on its own."

Ndi sat transfixed as the suggestions ravaged his nerves. By the time he recovered from the shock, three customers came and sat down. That put an abrupt end to the conversation.

Chapter Fifteen

Ndi sat devastated like a person slapped on both jaws. And really, the two encounters that day were like slaps on his jaws. The, matron had blasted him in the morning for untoward language against his daughters and now, Enanga had brought in a loathsome forewarning – the possibility of losing his manhood in the accident and that of getting a girl from the ghetto and after raising her status, she turns out to be his suicidal weapon. That was a death knell. Either or both of the two predictions were worse than death.

It was still early evening, and he could not contemplate going back to his ward. Suppose he returned and the matron came back to chastise him once more? At the same time, his stay at the under-tree was proving as uncomfortable as going back. In short, the hospital environment in and out of the ward had become inhospitable to him. But the under-tree was better. There, people cracked jokes that distracted one from his main worries. So, he took courage and stayed on. Customers trickled in and gradually the place filled up.

Ndi admired the spirit of camaraderie with which the under-tree community greeted each other. They would rise in unison with open hands and embrace and hug a new comer as if he was returning from an overseas trip. Then they all would burst into a guffaw as if to purge themselves of previous days' quarrels and insults. As the pantomime of greetings was going on, there was a rattling noise coming from the main road. At first, nobody paid attention to it. But as it came nearer and louder, everybody turned to see what it was all about. And lo! It was the foul-mouthed once bastardized fellow shouting, "Nobody can beat me twice," and dragging a larger draughts board with him and challenging the craftsman who had beaten him in the game a few days back.

"Nobody can beat me twice. I sold nine human heads to acquire these skills. I am the alpha and the omega, the horizon that has no end, the September rains that respect no occasion, *o song o ngwe, o ngwe, ngwe*. He who treads on me treads on glowing magma. I challenge the under-tree community especially this fool who claims to have beaten me once, to a game of draughts. I shall bastardize any idiot who will dare look straight into my forehead," the fellow shouted.

The master craftsman whom the fellow targeted sat unruffled. The fellow moved onto him provokingly and placed the board on his legs.

"If you pretend not to hear me, know I am addressing myself to you. I challenge you. The other day, I was ill prepared. Come on, if you dare, if your mother did not deliver you on a rainy day, come on. You'll be disgraced now, you fool."

"My friend, you are joking with fire. I shan't play with you until the exchange of currency is complete. I still respect and mourn the gradual loss of the British pound;" the master craftsman said and put the board away."

"That's escapism. The French franc is as good. Let our fans bet. Give your money to a referee. I challenge you," he said and placed the board on his legs again.

The master craftsman took the challenge and beckoning Ndi declared him the referee and gave two thousand francs to him. "Give yours also and let's start," he challenged.

The fellow sulked. "We are not here to display money. We are here to display skills in draughts. It's five hundred francs."

"OK, five hundred, poor thing."

"Take; you amateur," the fellow slammed the first move.

"Take, empty-mouthed fellow," the craftsman responded with a blocking tactics.

The fellow looked confused as he risked losing several pieces if he made a wrong move.

"Take, your **mami pima**," the fellow countered as he unblocked the trick.

"Give, your **papa pima**," Enanga interrupted and kicked the board out of their hands sending the pieces flying all over.

"Enanga be careful e, I am not playing with you e, that nonsense that you do to your husband you should limit it e, this is a public place e, before you were born women sold palm wine here e!" the fellow shouted, and threatened to beat up Enanga.

"Try that your rubbish and I shall send you sprawling on the floor. From today, I don't want to see you here, you rough work of nature. You come here and make noise, you don't even buy wine. All you do is to insult women your mami pima, your mami pima. Was your mother's pima responsible for your being handicapped? If it was, not all women's pimas were. Shit," Enanga insulted. The master craftsman stood and moved seat thus ending the game.

The whole under-tree community condemned the fellow for always insulting women and banned him from playing draughts with anybody until he apologized to the women and paid a fine of a jog of palm wine to the community.

Ndi felt pity for the fellow. Though his joke was offensive and caused the row, it had worked as a sort of shock absorber on Ndi's tortured mind. It had given him some respite by catapulting his mind from his worries for a short while, thus giving him the peace he badly needed. He put two and two together and decided to intervene on behalf of the fellow.

"Ladies and gentlemen, when two cocks are fighting in the presence of a third, the third intervenes and stops the fight. I want to stop this row by paying the fine for my friend. Madam, give a jog of wine. Here is money – four thousand francs," Ndi said and gave the elderly woman money.

"No, madam, we want that fellow to pay the fine himself. A child that is carried never knows the stakes of the distance. He must pay the fine even if it takes him one year to do so. We are not in a hurry," one of the persons said.

"Mr. Ndachu, do you think you and Enanga can swallow me? You are small," the fellow blasted and dashed off whining like a dog.

"That's how those husks are – people who have been sold in cults; mouthy and provocative and when they offend one and one pushes them even slightly, they fall down and die, and the whole world shouts that one has killed a human being. That fellow is a living dead. His father sold him in the Hammock cult. We should be careful with how we deal with him," Mr. Ekendem revealed.

"Yes, that is what those rich people do. There is no rich man whose hands are clean. Their hands are always soaked in blood. The father of that fellow was just a groundnut seller at down beach near Kingsway. One day his third wife, the youngest, who begot that fellow died suddenly for no apparent reason. Before people forgot, his first son with his first wife died. Shortly after the two deaths, we saw him buy a plot. Before long, he built a fantastic house and bought a car. Then he started opening stores all over the place. People started pinching themselves as they questioned the sources of his wealth. As gossip has it, he tried to kill that fellow too but was unable because the fellow's maternal uncles fortified him. You know how tough those Bakossi people are. He succeeded only in maiming the boy. Because he could not kill him, he drove him away, accusing him of being a wizard," the eldest woman chipped in.

"Mamiyo, I tell you, there is a naked case like that in Tiko. My elder sister's friend told her that there is a man in Tiko whose source of wealth is very questionable. They say he was a plantation-hand. Then all of a sudden, he bought and moved house to Likumba Senior Service Quarters in a five bedroom house. They say the man sold his first wife's womb to a certain spirit called Beelzebub to become rich. The poor woman has no child till today. All her labour is being enjoyed by other women. I tell you, those rich people are terrible. I can never allow my daughter marry a rich man," one of the women said as she served Mr. Esoka a glass of wine.

Ndi scanned the woman from toe to head. He did not remember meeting her anywhere before the under-tree encounter. Was she referring to him? The story she told was patchy but the major elements were reminiscent of his. Was she talking about him? Sweat sprouted all over his body. Gall jetted into his mouth, he spat out what he could and swallowed what he could not. Undefined guilt made him withdraw from the under-tree community.

Chapter Sixteen

The day was very hard on Ndi. It had left a very painful impression on him. He returned to the ward shaken and thought of mending fences with the matron. But how would he approach her? Would he lie that he had forgiven his wives? Would he say he had moderated his stand on his daughters? How will they start the conversation? And who would take the initiative? "OK," Ndi said to himself, "if she comes I shall feign serious pains and I know she would be concerned and start the conversation". But when the matron came Ndi lost track of his strategy.

"Good evening Mr. Ndi," the matron greeted. How was your day?"

"Not bad at all. I was wheeled to the road and I had some fun with palm wine drinkers. The people are very funny."

"That's great. How has the boy been doing? Is he of service to you?"

"Very well, very serviceable. I admire him."

"That's good. I shall be on mission tomorrow. We are going for a conference in Yaounde and when I return I shall be on leave. So, you will have another team of nurses and a matron to take care of you. I have prepared all your documents for a meticulous follow up. Next week, you will be X-rayed to see whether it is time for you to start training to walk on your own. Be truthful to the nurses because they have to report your exact situation to the doctor. I believe your rehabilitation will take a month or so and you will be allowed to return. So, take care."

"Matron, I pray to have another team like yours. I am so indebted to you. May God take you safely to and fro your mission."

Saying that, Ndi shut his eyes and fell prey to a bout of hiccough. The matron understood the emotional concerns and tapped him on the back and left. The next day, Ndi made new acquaintances with the new team. Two days later he was X-rayed and after the results were made known, he was placed on the rehabilitation list. He co-operated with the rehabilitation unit and went through the three stages in record time. He was first introduced to standing in-between two cross bars, then using them as aids to walking, and finally he was given crutches. At every stage he performed well and before long he was discharged from hospital.

Ndi returned home to an empty house. His third wife had abandoned house before Mr. Ndeb told her of the divorce. In going, she took all her children with her to her maternal brother's house in Tole. Although Ndi had sent word that he did not want to meet her in his house upon his return from hospital, he was ill prepared for the loneliness that greeted him when he got home. Agreed, he hardly pampered his daughters before he was taken to hospital. But he was used to the noise they made, the running up and down and childish temper that flared up and cooled down with no apparent reasons. All that, was now lost. In the first week, Mr. Ndeb's wife provided him with food. But with time, she started complaining and making derogatory remarks about people who divorced wives. From disparaging remarks she started preparing food that Ndi said he did not like. Her relationship with him got sourer and sourer until he realized that she did not want him. When Mr. Ndeb called her to order, she asked him whether Ndi's wives were sick – "a man who divorces one woman would divorce another and so has no right to eating food prepared by a woman. If I gave him food within the first few days of his return from hospital, it was because I was obliged by common human concerns for one another."

"OK, then I shall not also eat your food," Mr. Ndeb threatened.

"Thank God. Shall I now go falling from waterfalls because you have refused eating my food? That will give me some respite. The woman is the only creature that works without leave. Thanks for my leave. Don't eat."

Mr. Ndeb did not eat his wife's food that day. The next day, he thought she would reconsider her stand. That day, she prepared delicious *quacoco*, popularly known as *timba-na-mbusa*, her husband's delicacy. To his surprise she prepared very little of it – in fact for only herself and the children. When they were eating the eldest daughter whom her husband called mother because she was named after his mother, and whom he pampered to a fault refused to eat because her father was not given food.

"Mr. Man," Mrs. Ndeb addressed her husband. "Your daughter has refused eating. What do I do with her? If she does not eat, I shall give her food to Ndeb junior. I see he still has good appetite."

Mr. Ndeb eyed her scornfully, withdrew from the scene and went to the club. He ordered for fried chicken and banana and while he ate, Ndi came in and ordered for the same dish. The food was delicious but expensive. Some people called it pay-day food because they could only afford it on pay-days.

"Baa," Mr. Ndeb addressed Ndi. "I must apologize for my wife's very poor conduct. She has never behaved like that before. But it seems to me that it is mere woman solidarity. Else, I don't know what has prompted her to behave as she has. You know her very well. She is a welcoming woman. Please let me foot our two bills."

"That is not necessary. I prefer footing the bills for one thing, I can't blame your wife. Do you remember that I told you when you visited me in hospital that I had things to tell you when I returned from hospital? Let me tell you now, my first wife is my undoing. Everything around me is in her control. As we are conversing here now, she is eavesdropping on our conversation and giving her lieutenants instructions on what to do with me. Although I hear she is in Bamenda, distance does not hinder her from doing what she wants to do anywhere. To her, distance does not exist. Fai Nchotu told me that she was the wife of Beelzebub, the second most powerful evil spirit. He said she had begotten eleven children, all boys in the spirit world before she took human form; and that was why she could not have children in this world. He added that she was the main source of my wealth and would disappear with it the day she would decide to return to the spirit world by sloughing her physical being. So, whatever your wife is doing is not of her making. She is simply under the directives of Queen Beelzebub."

Mr. Ndeb screwed his face as if in sympathy with Ndi then he asked him an embarrassing question. "Do you believe in such things? That is mean superstition."

"Baa," Ndi addressed him. "Am I a child? Let me tell you, if you are not superstitious, you cannot be a Christian. Superstition is the other side of Christianity and vice versa. You can't talk of positive without thinking of negative. When a seer says, who dares say the contrary?"

"Man, Fai Nchotu has destroyed so many families. He has put so many people at daggers drawn that, the other day, he was arrested for provoking a fight between two brothers because he said one was bewitching the other. So be careful with what he told you. If that is what has influenced your actions you should reconsider them," Mr. Ndeb said with a firmness that compelled Ndi to make a quick review of how he had lived with his wives.

His first wife was the daughter of his father's friend. She was betrothed for him by his father who knew the ins and outs of his wife's family. All his relatives had recommended the marriage and had staked whatever they had on it. Both families were Christian families though not very obsessed. He had not suspected his wife of evil doing even under the difficult situation of being barren. She had never asked him to consult a seer. She had never on her own gone to see one. None of her friends had been accused of belonging to a cult. None of her friends had accused her of belonging to a cult. She had readily yielded to his demand to marry another woman. Upon the marriage she sacrificed all she could for the new wife's comfort. The only person who had accused her of being evil was Fai Nchotu. And now, Mr. Ndeb was saying Fai Nchotu was fake. He was a liar who destroyed families with his lies. Was it that that was what has happened to him? Has Fai Nchotu destroyed his family? If that was the case, what will he do – go begging the divorced wives to come back? The answers to these questions were too much for him. He ate fast and returned to his house with the intention of putting his jigsaw puzzle together and finding a solution. But immediately he got home, the environment recreated the dreadful scene of his predicament. He saw in his mind's eyes the unfolding of the drama that led to his being admitted in hospital - how he tried to woo his third wife into weaning their three- months-old baby, the ground nuts his first wife gave him and he refused to eat them, the slap he gave her, and worse of all, his third wife's violence on him.

Ndi turned livid with undefined thoughts. He could not see clearly where to lay blames for his problems. So long as he was concerned, he was blameless. His first wife, if judged from the point of view of physical nature was blameless also; but from the point of view of her spiritual nature (that was of course, beyond the comprehension of the common

83

man) she could not be exonerated. Judged from the two points of view, his third wife was blameless from the spiritual point of view, but was blameful from the physical, as evidenced by her violence. So, neither of the women was worth the pain and rituals of being asked to return. And with that, he brushed aside Mr. Ndeb's plea for him to reconsider his decision to divorce his wives. He thought the only problem he had was keeping the house clean and fetching water if the taps went dry. The club provided a variety of delicious foods and he could rely on having food from there until he got a new wife. So, he got one of his company's hands, and made him house-help.

Chapter Seventeen

The first three months of Ndi's return from hospital were uneventful. He recovered steadily, and was proud he was bouncing back. But the forth month was crammed with very demanding activities. The sea ports of Tiko and Victoria were losing grounds to that of Douala. In fact they were virtually being put out of action as Buea was winding up being capital of a once politically significant entity. Southern Cameroons businessmen were frantically transferring their Head Offices to Douala. To prevent carpets and other office equipment from being stolen by workers, as they were being stolen in Buea government offices by heads of different government departments, Ndi supervised the parking, loading and escorting vehicles carrying the things to Douala. He could make two to four trips to Douala a day. That kept him so busy that he forgot about wives and other concerns.

One day, he returned from Douala very late. He had not eaten the whole day. He went to the club but found nobody there, it had closed. He was dead hungry. The whole place was quiet. He returned to his house, swallowed spittle a couple of times and went to bed. The next morning he vowed to end his loneliness by looking for a wife. He called one of his company's hands and confided in her his desire to marry a Bamenda girl from a poor background. He gave her specific instructions and allowance and commissioned her to comb the Miselele, Mundoni and other CDC camps for a suitable virgin.

"Should the girl be beautiful?" the envoy asked.

"She shouldn't be a cripple," Ndi responded.

"Of what educational background?" she asked.

"Not completely illiterate. At least capable of counting one to ten million francs, can sign her name, and capable of being taught to handle business records," Ndi responded.

"OK, Standard six."

"That won't be bad. So long as she is a virgin. You see, Tiko girls are terrible. I don't want an express road of a girl with the possibility of coming to marriage double."

"OK, Sir. I see you as soon as I find one. Only a girl from Bamenda!"

"Most preferably."

The envoy left and after three days search, she came to report her findings. She had seen the daughter of an Overseer at Mundoni oil processing plant. She was light in complexion, ended in standard four and had no prospects of furthering her education because of her mother's illness that was ruining the family financially.

On hearing the description of the girl and why she could not further her education, Ndi's heart leapt up with joy. Saliva oozed into his mouth, he spat out what he could and swallowed what he could not.

"When do we go and see her and her parents?"

"It depends on you. If you say now, fine."

"What about Sunday? Sunday is ideal. We have to carry some gifts to her and her parents."

"OK, Sir. Sunday," the envoy said and left.

On Sunday they went and made the first contact with the girl's family. At first, the family feigned disinterestedness complaining of the age difference and fearing the children of Ndi, some of whom were older than their daughter.

"How can they turn hostile in a home in which they don't belong? They will get married and go to their husbands. Debora will be in my home and will have total protection. Who will challenge her in my house? Will the person be crazy?

"OK, as you say. Man proposes but God disposes," the father of the girl said out of ignorance rather than out of the meaning of the proverb; then added as of an after thought, "What God has planned nobody can scatter."

After what looked like a jolly good time, Ndi and the envoy returned to Tiko in very high spirits. Just for that apparently successful contact with his would be family in-law, Ndi promoted the envoy to the lucrative post of chief cashier in charge of the Bonaberi main hardware store. And with that the two coordinated their efforts and within a few weeks Ndi married his forth wife – a virgin from Mundoni Oil Mill. He carefully wrote down the date and time of their first sexual encounter.

Ndi was overjoyed when in that first night with his wife he did not falter. He had all along been afraid of Enanga's ominous forecast that the accident could cost him his manhood. He was thankful to God that he was full of vigour. And if God retained his manhood it meant He would give him his heart's desire. And as the saying goes, 'strike the iron while it is hot', he went headlong into striking his iron while it was red hot. In the morning he beamed with smiles. His wife had proven beyond all doubts that she was well brought up. To prove to her and her parents that he was grateful he offered more than the deflowering pig. Lorry loads of gifts accompanied the pig to Mundoni. And for two days running, the camp was en fete. And everybody that participated in the fete, prayed for God's mercy on the couple. And verily, verily in three months Debora's accelerated grow with her first contact with a man, was complemented with a complexion change.

Ndi was hilarious but confused. He did not know where to put his faith. He thought of going to see Fai Nchotu to ask him about the sex of his expected baby. But when he remembered what Mr. Ndeb had told him about Fai, he decided to go to church and take a seven day novena prayer with a three day dry fast end. He complemented the prayer with unimaginable alms to the church and the poor, and other works of charity. He poured love and gifts on his wife. Debora had some childhood blemishes on her body probably caused by insect bites and scratches caused by wild grass as she fetched firewood in the plantation. The blemishes tended to grow more conspicuous and disfiguring as she built up flesh. The Tiko/Douala road had just been completed thus giving easy access to Douala. To treat the blemishes, Ndi frequently took her to Douala where a Bonanjo-based Dermatologist prescribed highly fragrant and very expensive body lotions. The lotions played a double roll – treating the blemishes and enticing Ndi. He became so obsessed to the fragrance that he always wanted to drive along with her. Sometimes he drove her to Buea to see the phasing out of a once teeming capital city of Southern Cameroons. At the height of pampering her, he took her to luxurious hotels especially Akwa Palace Hotel and gave her sumptuous treats. He employed four house-helps to attend to her. In the sixth month, he flew her to France for preparatory shopping. Unfortunately for him, it turned out that he could only do shopping for her, not the child since he did not know the sex of the child.

Debora's pregnancy developed normally. She was smart and healthy. But every passing month made Ndi very anxious and depressed. Sometimes he would want to keep a good distance from his wife. He tended to attribute close proximity with bad news and so tried to keep away as if bad news could be altered by distance. At the approach of the month he considered to be the eighth month of pregnancy, his anxiety worsened and he became hypertensive. When the month came and passed by relieving him of his fears, he became more relaxed and hopeful. He became more attached to his wife. He showered her with love. Debora returned the love with childish charm. Towards the middle of what he thought was the ninth month, he feigned excessive work demands and moved to Douala after arranging and handing over the care of his wife to two doctors at Cottage Hospital Tiko. His only link with his wife then was Radio Buea. Every morning and afternoon he listened to the radio programme announcing births. At about the end of what he thought was the ninth month; his extreme anxiety came back. He glued his radio on his ear. But a small distraction cost him the news. And so, he missed when the radio announced that his wife had given birth to a bouncing baby girl.

Debora's parents went wild with jubilation. According to them, any girl who started childbearing with a baby girl had great prospects of not only begetting many children but also of begetting more boys than girls. As such, they took their largest *njangi* group women to Tiko to sing the praises of Ndi and his wife. On arrival at Tiko however, they were stunned when they were told that Ndi was in Douala running his businesses. That revelation terrified the Mundoni women. They considered Ndi's displacement at that time, irresponsibility. They doubted how a responsible and experienced man could abandon an inexperienced girl giving birth for the first time to herself in the pretext that she had been entrusted into the hands of competent doctors. They asked whether the businesses were worth their daughter's life. Mr. Ndeb saw the tension build up and so dispatched somebody to Radio Buea to make another announcement.

Ndi heard the announcement this time but missed getting the sex of the child. He rushed to Tiko and met passive, virtually depressed women sitting on doorsteps and stones, resting their chins in their palms as if in mourning. Nobody ran to welcome him and hug him. So he assumed that if the child did not die, then it was a girl. On asking, he was told his wife had given birth to a bouncing baby girl. He at once mistook the mourning atmosphere for sympathy with him on the birth of his eighth daughter. He moved to his sofa and sat in it with folded hands to complement the mourning. His parents in-law took that as a confirmation of nonchalance and abandoning their daughter to the forces of death.

Mr. Ndeb called Ndi out of earshot and told him about the charged atmosphere and the necessity to diffuse it. He told him about the gossip and promised to help appease the in-laws. He then advised him to feign illness and fatigue and take some aspirin in the open to confirm that. Ndi gave him the go ahead and took the aspirin as advised.

Mr. Ndeb then went in for the attack. He had organized Tiko women in a house several houses away from Ndi's compound. He shrieked, and after a drawn interval the women started shouting, ululation, singing and dancing. The people in Ndi's compound thought there was a birth celebration in the compound. But soon the singing and dancing came closer and closer to Ndi's compound. The women sang:

Solo:	If in-laws will not sing,
Chorus:	We shall sing,
Solo:	If in-laws will not dance,
Chorus:	We shall dance,
Solo:	If in-laws are not joyous,
Chorus:	We are joyous,
Solo:	When in-laws see us singing,
Chorus:	They should sing,
Solo:	When in-laws see us dancing,
Chorus:	They should dance,
Solo:	When in-laws see us joyous
Chorus:	They should be joyous

At that, the singing women made a loud noise. The visiting women reciprocated with a welcoming reconciliatory shout and the two groups merged in singing and dancing. Ndi thanked Mr. Ndeb for that reconciliation.

Chapter Eighteen

If the birth of a daughter was disappointing to Ndi, his wife's emerging beauty more than counterpoised it. Debora was emerging as a veritable majestic and stately woman, a stateliness that caught the eye of many a man. With the birth of her child, she seemed to have sloughed her blemished old skin. It seemed as if the pre-birth nutrition had laid a dormant layer of fat just beneath the skin which now was moistening greasing and glazing oils that made her skin flicker as if tiny grains of crystal were sprinkled on it. Debora now a master craftswoman in cosmetics embellished that natural splendour with the numerous body lotions she had. Her flesh responded favourably to the treatment as it filled up the minutest depressions on the body. With that dazzling and tantalizing beauty – beauty some people described as beyond human evaluation, Ndi learnt to cut his T's and dot his I's. In other words, he learnt to fit himself within the new context by at least feigning to appreciate his daughter and shower his wife with love.

Many people thought Debora's beauty made Elizabeth Makeba's (former Miss Nigeria) beauty look paltry by comparison. If one shook hands with her or embraced her, he carried her fragrance for days. In the fifth month of delivery, her parents wanted her to come and 'rest' with them at Mundoni. Debo, as she was fondly called at that time, was very anxious to return to her birth place to nurse her child with her parents for a brief while. When she proposed it to Ndi, he opposed the idea. He said he feared her treated blemishes could reappear with a little carelessness and that he did not like the child to be exposed to unfavourable natural or man-made forces at that early age. Debo was easily convinced. She thus invited her mother to move over to Tiko to give her a motherly helping hand which the house-helps lacked. Ndi was forced to accept the proposal though it did not appeal to him.

Debo had a baby girl, yes. She was unearthly beautiful, yes. She was in the fifth month of nursing, yes. The child had an array of cow and cereal products for food, and so her survival did not depend on breastfeeding, yes. Ndi was anxiously looking for a next of kin, yes. If his mother in-law were not living with them and sharing the same room with his wife, he could start manoeuvring her for weaning the child, yes. So, if his house were not conducive for a new start in love-making, Douala would, yes. And so, Ndi formed the habit of driving his wife to Douala in order to seduce her into weaning the child. He would give her unending treats in luxurious hotels, buy her expensive jewellery and on their return, he would tell her how it was necessary for them to have a boy who would be his next of kin.

"If I don't have a boy, a next of kin with you, you will see, my brothers will drive you out of my estates. But if you secure yourself with a son, you'll have all. You know in Bamenda, women don't inherit either their husbands' or their fathers' estates," he said.

"Yes, but my mother told me that a child is weaned at two years." Debo responded.

"When the child has already grown a beard? Aren't those things of old?" Ndi asked with suppressed anger.

"Yes, but that is what she said. She said in Bamenda, people avoided early weaning by marrying many wives."

"So, you want me to marry many wives?"

"No; my mother says, I should tell you that we should marry in church."

"Marry in church? Church means monogamy, therefore early weaning of children. Furthermore, children of nowadays don't breastfeed. They drink milk."

"So, what do you want me to do?"

"We have to wean the child."

"OK, I shall tell my mother."

"Why? Are you not a mother yourself? How can one mother tell another mother what she wants to do?"

The conversation ended abruptly as Debo pouted as if something disgusting had been suggested to her. Ndi did not want to offend her. He knew the odds were against him, so he had to play his cards well. When they got home, he defused the tension with a series of jokes. His mother in-law responded with her own jokes. The evening wore on well and at bed time, the family went to bed.

At night Ndi could not sleep. He reviewed his wife's childish and apron-string relationship with her mother. He remembered that girls with such attachments to their mothers always posed problems to their husbands because they reasoned through their mothers and behaved as if they were doubles of their mothers. If his wife insisted on church wedding, things would be difficult on him because there would be impediments to his marrying another wife if she did not have a son with him. On the other hand if he refused church wedding he could lose his Perl of great beauty. So, what would he do with that impasse?

Several solutions came into his mind. He thought he could make his wife realize that it was in her best interest to wean the child and look for a boy. If that appeal failed, he would use hostesses to lace her juices with cognac and when she got tipsy, rape her. If that failed, make her jealous by taking her to night clubs, abandoning her and dancing with other girls. If that failed, brave her mother and tell her to lord it on her to accept his proposal. If that failed, threaten divorce. With that polluted mind, Ndi woke up in the morning completely devastated. That day, he did not take his wife to Douala and on his return, did not bring any gifts. When she heard the revving of the car, she rushed to welcome him. She embraced him, hugged him and kissed him in the manner she saw white and Douala women kiss their husbands in hotels. After Ndi had rested and eaten, he went to the club. While away, Debo's mother scolded her for kissing her husband.

"Who told you that a nursing mother kisses her husband? Suppose you work him up, what will you do? Or, have you started doing it already since you go to Douala everyday? You don't breastfeed your child. Everyday, cow milk, everyday cow mild. Did you deliver the child for the cow to feed her?"

"Mama, modern children drink only cow milk. Breastfeeding makes women old quick. My husband has the money to buy milk. What is your problem?"

"Look, I shall not want to bear witness to your getting pregnant prematurely. The rubbish you are saying is telling. A nursing mother does not dress the way you dress. She does not go out with her husband the way you go. Your perfumes are most enticing. I don't like that. I don't like it. Only the house-helps carry your child. How will your child know and love you if you don't carry and breastfeed her for her to identify you from your scent? What do you think makes chickens know their mothers? It is brooding — brooding makes them acquainted with the scent of their mother and vice versa."

"OK, mama. OK, I have heard."

Ndi had told his driver before he went to the club not to come for work the next day. It was customary that whenever he wanted to take along his wife to Douala he drove himself. Since he wanted to take her to Douala the next day, he told the driver not to come to work. In the morning, he told his wife to get ready to go to Douala.

94

"I want to remain with the baby. She has been missing me and I have been missing her. If it weren't imperative for you to go to work, I would have suggested that we take care of the child today."

Ndi screwed up his brows, trembled in anger, whined like a dog, entered his car and dashed off, creating a cloud of dust that gust into the compound and house. It took some time for the dust to dissipate.

"Why is your husband driving away in such anger," Debo's mother asked.

"I don't know. It may be because he is late."

"What about his driver, where will he meet him?"

"I don't know."

"If I had my way, I would have stopped him and advised that he goes for his driver. It is not good to drive in anger," Debo's mother remarked.

Chapter Nineteen

Debo and her mother soon forgot about Ndi and settled onto taking care of the child. For the first time, she had the feel of personal child-caring. She curdled the child, bathed her, and fed her though with canned milk. When the child fell asleep, she proudly lay down with her. When they got up, her admiring mother remarked, "Can you imagine that? What you have done, what you have experienced, especially if you had complemented it with breastfeeding, is the essence of motherhood, money cannot buy it. All human relationships are based on it. It is priceless. There are thousands of women longing for that experience but they cannot have it." On her part, Debora full of herself, exhaled and released her satisfaction with, "It is wonderful mama". From then, the two shuttled the baby between them and forgot about any other thing in life. Their day proved rather short and so the evening came prematurely. By 10 o'clock, nothing seemed abnormal. At midnight, Debo started; Ndi had not returned. Did he decide to spend the night in Douala? It was late for her to go and ask Mr. Ndeb if Ndi had told him he would spend the night in Douala. So, she consoled herself with the thought that he might have decided to spend the night in Douala.

Early in the morning, she went and asked Mr. Ndeb whether her husband had told him that he would spend the night in Douala. Mr. Ndeb shook his head and said, "No".

"Where should he be then? He did not return. Yesterday, he left in anger because I refused to accompany him to Douala. It may be he has ended up in another woman's house. Yes, he has; else where is he? Let him return, I shall see where he will enter. I swear to God, he will not enter my house today," she lambasted and returned in a whirlwind.

Since she did not give Mr. Ndeb the chance to respond, he followed her to her house and advised her to calm down. He said he did not think of anything abnormal. He had listened to Radio Buea, but there was no accident announced along the Tiko/Douala road that day, so, he believed Ndi might have spent the night in Douala to catch up with work because of the on-coming national day. That response clicked open Debo's mind. On the one hand she feared the possibility of an accident, on the other; she thought her husband spent the night in Douala to catch up with work. The fear of the possibility of an accident was dispelled by the fact that Radio Buea did not announce any accident along the Tiko/Douala road. So, she eased up with the belief that her husband had spent the night in Douala to catch up with work.

Just as the family settled on that and started going about their daily cores, news filtered in that a car wreck reminiscent of Ndi's car was discovered a good distance from the main road in a ravine about a kilo meter on the French Cameroon side of the Mungo bridge. There was blood in the wreck but the driver and passengers were not found. The driver seemed to have skidded off the road and hit an embankment that propelled the vehicle over the gutter without leaving a telltale trace. Thus several people passed by without noticing that there was a car in the ditch fifty meters from the road.

When Mr. Ndeb got the news, he did not hide it from Debo. He told her straight but cautioned her against overt manifestation of grief before they knew what had happened. Then he asked one Mr. Sone a Field Assistant, to allow them the use of his car. The three immediately left for the scene. They identified the wreck as Ndi's car but were confused on where his remains would be.

"Since this is French Cameroon territory, I believe we should go to Bonaberi police station and inquire," Mr. Sone suggested. There was no gainsaying. They left for the police station and there the police told them that at around six o'clock last evening, a truck driver came to report to them that there was an accident along the Douala /Tiko road. According to him, he saw a car at top speed driving on the wrong side of the road. When he realized that the driver was driving into him for a head-on collision, he horned and slammed his breaks. The driver, who was apparently drunk or lost in thoughts, panicked and lost control of the vehicle, and started swerving from left to right, and skidded into a ravine. Unfortunately there were no people around to help. So, he, the driver of the truck rushed to ask for police intervention. They, the police immediately rushed to the scene and forced open the car door to rescue the driver. He was alone in the car. He was taken to the district hospital in a coma. Mr. Ndeb, Debora and Mr. Sone dashed off to the district hospital. At the hospital, they met Ndi abandoned in a squalid veranda of what was called the emergency ward. The ward was full to the brim and so new patients were left at the veranda. The combined smells of coagulated blood several weeks old, drainage system that had ruptured in several places into which rats shuttled with impunity and patients' rags made breathing extremely difficult. Ndi had been laid on a bench with a sachet of dribs hanging on a nail in a wall with pealing paint.

Debora's aura transformed the atmosphere in the hospital as the guilt of the surrounding caused the dazzled doctors and nurses to rush to ask whether Ndi was her patient. She did not respond. She stood in her majesty in mute concern as she fixed a million watt gaze on Ndi. After a brief while, she turned, and with a voice irked with contempt, asked the doctors whether she could carry the patient away.

"You can, but you will have to fill discharge forms."

"Would death have filled the forms? Isn't this treatment a way of condemning a patient to death? See, your drip stopped dripping and there was nobody to reactivate it. Should we leave the patient here for you to complete what the accident did not?" Mr. Ndeb asked angrily and led Debora in signing the discharge forms. After that they carried their patient to Victoria hospital. Ndi's old doctors worked frantically on him. They discovered that apart from the gash across his forehead, his once treated spine was dislocated in several places and wondered whether he would be able to walk again on his own. Several days later, Ndi recovered full consciousness and asked where he was. Debo told him he was in hospital. He had had an accident and was admitted in hospital.

Chapter Twenty

Ndi remained in hospital for six months under intensive care – six months of premonition, six months of agony, and six months of nondescript feelings. The doctors did the best they could to ease his pains and comfort him but he was not only in physical pains, he was in a quagmire of psychological pains. Debo had broken the barrier of earthly beauty and whenever she visited her husband in hospital the mesmerized doctors and male nurses tended to lavish attention on Ndi. Female nurses were cowed by her presence. Some people accused her of over-dressing and making a mockery of her husband's accident. They said she came to hospital to advertise herself and not to take care of her husband. Ndi tended to agree with that and responded to the doctors' and nurses' concerns with sighs or moans. But the plain truth was that whatever dress Debo wore, made of her such a stately majesty of height and bearing that onlookers were compelled to bow in veneration. Furthermore, her husband had bought her so many expensive dresses that she could wear a different dress a day for one year.

One day she brought their one year one month old child to hospital. Ndi saw the replica of his wife and sighed. He screwed his brows and thought it was the best time he would have been weaning the child. But there he was, condemned to a wheelchair. He remembered the proverb that, a light in complexion woman is like roasted pork, you can hide the meat but not hide the scent, and even if you don't eat the pork, you'll 'eat' the scent. The thought of his wife being roasted pork around town turned him inside out. He remembered Enanga's ominous prediction and regrettably acknowledged that the accident had put an end to his ambitions. He was now, a living corpse. As he thought over this, he sighed and sighed again.

In the sixth month, he was discharged from hospital. He returned to a hilarious welcome by the people of Tiko and Mundoni. Yet to him, he returned to a world of no consequences, a world that was worse than death. Time and again he told his sympathizers that it would have been better if he had died.

"No, no matter how useless life is, it is better than death because in life, there is hope; in death there is no hope," one of the visitors remarked.

"Death sooths the pain of useless life," Ndi responded emphatically.

"That is mere conjecture," the fellow intervened again.

Ndi turned his back and ended the conversation.

The untoward criticism of Debo's dressing made her go in for secondhand clothing to give her a shabby look. The dress she bought was a Cecil Gil mode thrown in course of time in a junk bail. On Sunday she wore it and went to church. Thinking she was shabby and nobody would take note of her, she moved right to the front of the church and sat down. After mass, all hell broke loose as women crowded around her to tell them the seamstress who had sewn or the shop in which she had bought the dress. No woman believed her when she said it was an *okirica*. She returned from church disgusted and angry and as she sighed and spoke to herself, she drew Ndi's attention to her. He saw his Perl in an unearthly radiance. He inhaled deeply and exhaled noisily. His heart beat fast; he developed a hiccough as he crawled to his bed, took a bottle of aftershave and swallowed its contents. A few minutes later, he was heard breathing heavily with glottal vibrations. Debo rushed to him and on discovering what was happening exclaimed and called Mr. Ndeb. Ndi soon slipped into a coma. Mr. Ndeb rushed him to the Cottage Hospital Tiko where he was diagnosed of swallowing a little quantity of a mild corrosive substance. The doctor and nurses worked hard and soon brought the situation under control. They put him in an exclusive intensive care unit where even his wife was not allowed to see him while investigations went on.

News spread that Ndi had died. His mother in-law rushed to Tiko to assist her daughter.

"What do they say is wrong with your husband?" She asked her daughter.

"I don't know. I returned from church angry with the Tiko women whose work is only to talk about me. Wherever I go, they make comments. So, when I returned, I met my husband sound and well. I don't know what happened with him. I heard him groaning very badly. So I called Mr. Ndeb and we carried him to hospital. He is there, he cannot speak."

"So, what are you doing? Have you seen whether he has money in the house? Go and gather all the valuable things he has, let me go and hide them before his people come else you will not see them when they come."

"I can't do that. Suppose he does not die and finds that things have been scattered in the house?"

"You will say, it was when you were crying and people were restraining you that things got scattered. In that way you can say, the people stole things."

"I shall not do that. If his brothers like they can come and take all the things."

Debo's mother stormed out of the house and returned to Mundoni. Not long after, the police summoned Debo to explain what happened with her husband. She narrated her part of the story and the police concluded that it was perhaps attempted suicide. They then suspended interrogations until Ndi himself was well enough to answer questions. When he was well enough to answer questions, he did not mince words. He told the police that he wanted to take his own life because he could not withstand what was going on around him.

"What is going on around you that you think has never happened to somebody else? Have you heard of the story of Job? There are thousands of cases like yours," the police advised and closed their investigations.

Mr. Ndeb was particularly angry. He told Ndi how they had suffered to bring him back to life after the Tiko/Douala road accident and how Ndi's attempted suicide was a slap on their faces. Ndi regretted his action and promised to bear his cross. Debo also expressed her anger. "Suppose you had died people would have said that I had poisoned you in order to inherit your property. That is what people say when an old rich man dies leaving a young wife behind."

Ndi sulked from shame and once more apologized. But there is one thing apologizing, and another abiding by the apology. So long as Debo was a grain of corn, and Ndi, a fowl with an abscess in the throat, there was a problem – an insurmountable problem. Ndi would go for days without food because of the inevitable alternative – divorce Debo or allow her have for him a next of kin by marriage. After all, there were invalids that begot children with their wives. Neither of the alternatives seemed feasible. Days, weeks, months and years passed on, Ndi remained adamant and emaciated under the weight of indecision.

Ndi's condition worsened everyday and even his friend Mr. Ndeb was becoming impatient with him. Debo on her part had shown remarkable courage to deal with a man who was starving himself to death. One day, Mr. Ndeb told her that their choir was chosen to represent the Tiko congregation in a rally in Tombel. They would be there for two days. The news struck her like a sledge harmer and she withered instantly.

104

"If you go then I am in trouble. I don't think he can last for another two days. He is wasting away these days at an alarming rate. I have not got the courage to talk to him," Debo said.

"Take heart, I believe I shall meet him alive. He's a jolly good fellow. He is quite resistant," Mr. Ndeb encouraged Debo and they parted.

Chapter Twenty One

Immediately Mr. Ndeb returned from the trip, he went to see Ndi. He met him convivial and sharp. While he was away, Debo had succeeded to convince Ndi to take some juice. He had taken it and some pap and that had reinvigorated him and made him think life was worth living after all. Mr. Ndeb was overjoyed when Ndi shook his hand and ended the handshake with the click of the fingers. Both the grip and the click were strong enough to indicate that Ndi was not dying.

"Baa, I am glad to return and meet you as strong as a stone. I am also thankful that your wife is as courageous as ever before. We went to Bakossi and there, I would say, what I found there prompts me to ask you questions which I would be grateful if you answered them sincerely. I want to ask you, have you ever been to Bakossi?"

"Yes, I worked there in the late fifties and early sixties first as a road construction labourer and then as a supervisor of bridge construction works. It was there that I brought my fortune. We built the Chonge Bridge and made a lot of money with the leftover material."

"Did you have any affairs with girls and women there?"

"Why not? As a young man and with plenty of money, we crossed several women there."

"After that had you any links with the women? That is, did you communicate with the women?"

"No. Once we left there and I plunged myself into business, I never had time to run around even within this vicinity. Why are you asking?"

"Because I saw a young man whose age is telltales of the time you say you were in Bakossi and most of all, he is a **carbon copy of you.** Here is his photograph. Take this photograph and swear by the gods, this is your son."

"Do you know the name of his mother?"

"Yes. He told me his mother is called Sophina."

"Did you ask his name?"

"Yes, he said he was called Ngweh."

"Massa, that's a long time ago. I wonder whether I can remember the names of the women I went out with in that area. But as you say, I shall look at the picture more keenly tomorrow and show it to one or two other people to assert if the person in it is my carbon copy," Ndi said and at once a mysterious sensation ran through him as he remembered what Fai Nchotu had told him.

Fai had been categorical in telling him that he, Ndi had a son. He, Ndi had refused it because he could neither imagine where nor link up at the time with Bakossi. It was like a ferry tale with an unimaginable achievement – too weird to be true. It made him lose all impressions; and deadened as he was, the evening and the night rolled by unnoticed. He could not remember whether he had slept or not. All he could remember was that he got up in the morning with a hazy desire to ask somebody to do something for him. But he could not remember what. Gradually his mind picked up and he sent a child to call Mr. Sone. When he arrived, Ndi showed him the picture.

"Mann!" Mr. Sone exclaimed. "There is nothing as wicked as age and worries. See what age and worries have made of you – saggy, rumpled and emaciated. But see you here as a young man – a tall, handsome and plump fellow. You were wonderful. You once lived. How and where did you get the picture?"

Ndi felt a tingling glow of pride overwhelm him. He suppressed overt manifestation of joy but went on to showing some other people the picture. After testing five other people and having the same reaction, he put the picture on the table intentionally for Debo who had been out to the market to see. Debo saw the picture with the blurred eyes of fatigue and passed to the room without comment. Ndi sighed in his heart and pushed the picture to the floor. When she came out of the room and saw the picture on the floor, she picked it up and seeing what it was exclaimed, "Massa, na you this? Unbelievable! You once lived. You were fantastic. That is how the world is."

"Which world are you talking about, ours or yours?"

"Both. Both worlds are the same in terms of destroying what there is," she responded and left. Ndi took the picture and hid it in his box.

Mr. Ndeb came to chat with him in the evening. He had wanted to give him time and not hurry him in showing people the picture. He met Ndi not explicitly excited but from every indication, there were signs of throbbing joy in his head. Mr. Ndeb started the conversation on a dry and farfetched topic and tried to dwell too long on it. Ndi showed his disgust with irregular and contradictory responses – questions where no questions were needed, exclamations where no exclamations were needed and so on. Mr. Ndeb got the message and changed topic.

"Baa, you have seen the picture. What is your reaction? Have you told your wife about it? What was her reaction?"

"Everybody takes the picture for my childhood picture. There is no gainsaying, even Debo acknowledged it as my childhood picture. So, from the picture, we can conclude that he is my son. But there is much more than that. You will have to go back to Bakossi and bring the boy here for me to see him and for us to have blood tests to ascertain that we are not on the wrong path. You will therefore have to go over the weekend so as to be present at your job on Monday. My Land Rover is at the Head Office in Douala. You will use it."

"How will you handle Debo on this?"

"While we are still at this stage of investigation, she need not know beyond having a hazy idea about the picture. So, when you are going, I shall send her to Mundoni to stay with her parents and help out her sick mother."

"I am in for a very difficult mission. I can't envisage a strategy I would use to dislodge that boy from his village. Where would I tell him, I am taking him to? If I say, to his biological father, suppose his mother had played tricks on somebody else and all along, the boy had taken the decoy for his biological father, won't that provoke him to violent reaction? You know Bakossi people. They are warriors. The boy may pose other problems, being unprepared, not having enough money and so on."

"You are very right but there are many ways you can circumvent the problems. We can take this as a path-finding mission by just going to create acquaintance. You go, find out about his mother, if she is still unmarried, things would be easier. If she is married, you approach her through intermediaries, and when you succeed in talking to her, be rest assured that you would succeed in talking to the boy," Ndi said and one week later, Mr. Ndeb set forth for Bakossi.

Chapter Twenty Two

M r. Ndeb incidentally got to Etahku village in Bakossi on a market day, and easily traced Ngweh in the market.

"I have come here purposely to see you and your mother. You will remember that last time we met in Tombel at the rally, I asked you to give me your picture because I wanted to find out something about you. I have done the findings and I want to see your mother. If you are not too busy, I shall like you to take me to her house."

Ngweh readily took Mr. Ndeb to his mother and returned to the market. After a brief while, Mr. Ndeb introduced himself and asked Sophina where her husband was.

"I am not married," she said.

"I am sorry, I thought my friend, your son's father was around," Mr. Ndeb said thus taking Sophina aback.

"Do I know where his father is? Do I even know whether he is alive? His father came here as a worker when they were building the Chonge Bridge and we fell in love. Then when I told him that he had impregnated me, he pouted and made promises and escaped. That is how men are especially graffi strangers."

"Can you make him out if you saw him? Can you remember his name? Mr. Ndeb asked.

"Why not? A man who has a child with me? How can I forget his name? It was not a one day affair. He could forget my name but I can't forget his. After all, sex takes place inside the woman but outside the man. And so the woman is more involved in it, and suffers more for its outcome. His name Joe Ndi rankles in me every time his son crosses my path."

111

"Madam, you sound hurt, very hurt. Do you think if he came here you would talk to him? Does he still mean anything to you?"

"How many years today? The time I was hurt is long past. The boy has grown and instead of being a liability he's a fantastic fellow, too mature for his age. He fends for himself and helps me considerably. So the time of bitterness is over."

"Mr. Ndi has sent me to see you and the boy. Are you ready to talk to me?"

"If you have come to see me, then you better eat before we talk. I thought you were just passing," Sophina said and quickly prepared food for Mr. Ndeb. After eating, he thanked her and started the conversation again.

"I have said Mr. Ndi has sent me to see you and the child because he wants him to visit him."

"Ah! He has now realized that he has grown and it's time to sell him in a cult? Else, what makes him want to see him? He wants to sell him in a cult and become rich. "

"It is not that. Ndi need not sell anybody in a cult before getting rich. He is already too rich. I think all he wants to do is to compensate for abandoning the child. I think he reproaches himself for punishing you and wants to mend fences. If you could accompany the boy, he would be grateful."

"Am I also his son? His son is in the market go and talk to him. If he accepts to follow you, fine. If he refuses, that is his business."

"You should not exclude yourself from the deal. You have played the role of his mother and father all along and any major step to upset that will need your blessing. So, I'll go and call him and leave the two of you to talk things over," Mr. Ndeb wound up, went to the market and brought Ngweh to talk to his mother. When Mr. Ndeb was about to leave the two of them to discuss, Sophina invited him to be present in her discussing the matter with her son. She asked

Mr. Ndeb to tell her son his mission. After he had done so, she told her son the story about his biological father then added:

"Ngweh, I named you after my father. The name Ngweh means counsellor. My father was a counsellor in every aspect of the word. He was rich and generous to a fault. He begot me alone, perhaps to the joy of his brothers who had expected to inherit his property. When I begot you, they became hostile and till date, their steaming hatred for you is manifested in the way they refer to you as *nchong* or *graffi*. But as God would have it, after I had suffered to bring you up without help from anybody, you grew up to be an exemplary boy. You dwarf all your age mates and even older fellows who grew up in the guidance of their fathers. Everybody in this village looks on you now for support, even those who deride you behind your back. I thank God for that and I believe you can be anything you would want to be. But now, this man before us has brought in what I may call an abscess in the mouth. You have heard what he has said. He has said your biological father wants to see you. Nobody has ever advised you to do things. You have always advised yourself on how to do your things. So, I leave you and your God to take the decision."

"OK. Let me go to the market and close my store. I shall not be long," Ngweh said and went to close his store. He returned with palm wine and offered it to Mr. Ndeb. The three of them drank it first in silence, and then, as if Mr. Ndeb thought that Ngweh was trying to play down his mission, he restarted the conversation. He reminded Ngweh why he had come and the necessity to dwell on that.

"I have heard what has brought you. I am just trying to think what time I shall give myself to go to Tiko and back. I have perishable things in my store. I need to liquidate them. I need to arrange several things before I move. So, I am not idle. Furthermore, you are going to sleep here, so, I have to arrange where you will sleep, all that is being worked in my mind."

Mr. Ndeb gasped with delight at Ngweh's wisdom. He soon left them and returned to close his store. Before he returned, he had made arrangement with one of his friends to allow Mr. Ndeb the use of his bed for the night. He also told the friend that he would travel the next day but did not disclose where and the aim of the mission. Upon his return, he told Mr. Ndeb and his mother that he was ready for the trip the next day. His mother did not like that easy acceptance. She suggested that Mr. Ndeb should return the next day and wait for Ngweh later. Ngweh argued that he did not want an undefined topic to disturb him for a long time. He wanted to go and return as soon as possible.

The next day, Mr. Ndeb and Ngweh set out for Tiko.

Chapter Twenty Three

Mr. Ndeb and Ngweh arrived Tiko late in the evening. To avoid bothering Ndi, they spent the night in Mr. Ndeb's house. In the morning, he went to see Ndi to tell him about the success of the trip and to find out how Debora would react if she saw Ngweh. He wanted as mush as possible to avoid confrontation. On inquiring about Debora, Ndi said he had asked her to go to Mundoni to help her sick mother. So, the atmosphere was conducive for the three to discuss. Mr. Ndeb then returned to bring Ngweh.

When Ndi saw Ngweh, he was overwhelmed by a mystical sensation that rendered him nervous for a brief while and finally inquisitive. He scrutinized every contour of the boy's body; saw the brand-marks of his family – the gap in the middle of the upper row of teeth, the twist in the left ear and the two projections that fell short of developing into full-fledged fingers on both last fingers; and exhaled with satisfaction. He immediately cancelled the idea of blood test. For sure, Ngweh was his biological son and therefore the only qualified child he could boast of, to be his next of kin. He raised his hand to shake Nweh's hand. Ngweh who did not know that his father was an invalid did not move close enough to have a firm grip and so only their fingers got in contact. Ndi adjusted his wheelchair and moved forward and thus had the satisfaction of a full grip. He held his son's hand for a long time, his heart throbbing with joy. When he released the hand he asked the boy to sit by his side. At that point, Mr. Ndeb left them.

Ngweh sat down with the stiffness of a robot facing the man who was claiming to be his father. Ndi remained silent for a long time dumfounded by seething guilt. He drew his nose and cleared his throat as he devised an appropriate approach to the conversation. He blew his nose and hiccoughed again and again, then rather confusedly, he started telling Ngweh his long story. Before he started telling the story, he apologized for any wrongs that might have been made. Then he unwound his life history. He told Ngweh everything – starting with how he went to Etahku as a young labourer and met Ngweh's mother, how he left the place without knowing that Sophina was pregnant, how he lost contact with her, how he made his money, his odyssey in marriage and daughter-bearing spree, his desire for a male heir, his two accidents that rendered him an invalid, his divorces and Debora the current wife, the discovery of Ngweh etc. etc. He apologized again for any mistakes made in the course of his life's evolution, and concluded that because in the Bamenda culture a woman cannot inherit her father's or her husband's homestead, he Ndi, having ascertained that he Ngweh, was his blood son, no matter what names society gave to sons and daughters begotten under the circumstances Ngweh was begotten, declares him (Ngweh) his rightful heir. He would therefore like Ngweh to move to Tiko for that declaration to be made public and legal before God and man. He added that because man was ephemeral and not in control of the forces of nature, he would want that to happen very fast because it required: elaborate legal procedures, introduction to companies and estates, and acquaintance with socio-cultural institutions and practices.

Ndi spoke for about one hour thirty minutes. While he spoke he observed Ngweh keenly. He found him intensely attentive and calculative but not excited with the prospects of inheriting great wealth. Ngweh's disposition remained unruffled; in fact it was difficult to determine his impressions. Ndi took that for a reaction against his abandonment and apologized once more. Ngweh's first body movement occasioning his verbal reaction to Ndi's story coincided with Mr. Ndeb's re-entry in the house.

"I have heard," Ngweh said in a flat and noncommittal voice. "What you have said requires not only elaborate legal and socio-cultural attention, but also a lot of reconciliation. I am ill prepared for that now because I have to return today. When I return, I shall prepare for a longer stay and then I shall tell you what I think."

Ndi felt very unkind vibrations in his brains. That was not what he expected. He had expected a jubilant Ngweh to leap up with excitement and enthusiasm and rush to hug him. But there he was, faced with a stonewall-response that was reminiscent of the matron's insistence on reconciliation. Reconciling with whom? He asked himself in his heart as he made a tunnel view of Ngweh.

"Do you say you will return today? I thought we shall be here for two days. What are you hurrying to do at Etahku? You liquidated your perishable goods. So, stay with us, let's have your feel," Mr. Ndeb persuaded Ngweh.

"The earlier I go back, the earlier I shall come back. My visit here has disrupted several of my plans. I have to reorganize myself for the un-envisaged trips I shall be making in future."

Ndi suppressed expressing a little growth of anger as he wondered what plans a village boy had that rendered him insensitive to glowing wealth. What, what on earth, knowing Bakossi and the village of Etahku, what makes Ngweh have such audacity, such apparent defiance of *bon être*? With partially drawn brows he asked him whether he was prepared to move to Tiko or not. "I want to know because as I have said, man is ephemeral. I don't give myself much time on earth anymore. But before I go, I must keep my house clean."

117

Mr. Ndeb predicted a rift and cut in, "I don't think that question is in place now because Ngweh has not dismissed your request. He simply says that he has not tidied up. A man is a man. He has promised to come back. My worry with him is that we have not received him as one should receive an august guest. I thought if he spent another night I shall show him how we live in Tiko. Unfortunately he insists on returning today. We shouldn't disturb him. Let him go. I expect to see him here soonest," Mr. Ndeb said, and with that they allowed Ngweh to return.

Ngweh's return plunged Ndi into melancholy. He was sceptical about the boy's interest in what he thought would entice any other young man. Mr. Ndeb quickly intercepted.

"You look withdrawn and at the verge of going on hunger strike again. But let me tell you, self-torment has no place here. If that boy were not to come here again, he would have told us straight. I have never seen a solid before-his-time boy like that – too mature for his age. His mother said his whole village depended on him for subsistence. Can you imagine that? Have you seen the maturity he has displayed here? Any other boy, especially one who was abandoned to fend for himself would have been euphoric at the prospects of great plenty. But he takes his time and suppresses untoward emotions. So, let's be hopeful. My worry is how Debora would receive him," Mr. Ndeb said.

"Who is Debora?" Ndi asked. "Is she the one who is still keeping me alive? Wasn't it her stiff necked-ness that ran me into the accident that has put an end to my life like this? Is she better than the other women? If that boy had given me unequivocal assurance, I would have told her in her face to leave my house. What is she to me but an artificial flower? Can I sow seeds with her again? Ours ended the day this accident happened, If she returns, I shall tell her the truth about Ngweh and if she likes, she can go hang," Ndi said, his voice vibrating with undefined anger.

"Avoid antagonizing people now. When she returns, tell her about Ngweh and see her reaction. Her reaction will determine how you will relate with her," Mr. Ndeb advised.

Two days later, Debora returned from Mundoni virtually spent. She had had it rough with her mother who bore her a grudge for not vandalizing her husband's house when he was comatose after the accident. Because of Debora's state, Ndi postponed telling her about Ngweh. The next day however he told her. He said the picture she once mistook for his childhood picture was in fact the picture of his son out of both traditional and modern wedlock. The son, whose name was Ngweh visited him while she was away at Mundoni. The boy would return to Tiko in due course to be declared his designated heir before the administration and the church.

"Will you leave his mother behind? Why don't you say you would marry his mother before he becomes your next of kin? That would make him more legal than if you heaved one illegality upon another illegality," Debora responded and moved away grumbling and threatening to return to her mother.

Ndi sighed and asked her, "Are those your threats aimed at derailing my plans? Or you think you are the one to tell me what is legal and what is not legal. I had expected your reaction and put it within the only option – return to Mundoni."

Debora did not respond but thought of confronting Mr. Ndeb whom she thought was in the known of Ndi's plans but hid them from her. And as sure as death, she confronted him. He defended himself and advised her to be calm. "Be calm Madam. You know your husband's outbursts are as the result of his situation. He is influenced by several things. So, when he utters an unkind word you should not respond," Mr. Ndeb said rather confusedly.

Debora was not satisfied. She made good her threats by abandoning house and returning to Mundoni. When she told her mother about Ndi's plan to install Ngweh as his heir, her mother leaped into the air and crashed onto the floor.

"Do you now see what I told you? What did I tell you? Didn't I advise you to take advantage of that man's accident and enrich yourself by carrying away one of the boxes of money he had in the house? You thought listening to the advice of an old woman was not worth the salt. Now where are you? Has an old man not ravaged your youth for nothing and you will return barehanded as you went? Who will marry you again? Even if one braved the odds and married you because of your beauty will he not say he is marrying a secondhand woman and so curl in, in every aspect of the marriage? Didn't I advise you to look for a young man and speculate on having a boy for that fool while he was still in a coma? You folded your buttocks with the lame excuse of being faithful to a thing rendered useless by a self-inflicted accident. Now look, you will not return to Tiko again until that man sends emissaries here whom I shall give conditions for your return. You will not return to a man who wants to install a crown bastard his heir. Did he not know about his bastard before coming to soil you? Or is it because he cannot mount you any more that he thinks you are useless to him and he can treat you with the least respect? A man in his state allows his wife to have children for him with a chosen young man. But because he is so presumptuous, so conceited he does not think that is the ideal way left for him now. If he considers a bastard more fit to inherit his property than his wife or his daughter, then you shall not return to him," Debora's mother decreed and that was it.

Chapter Twenty Four

Ngweh returned to Tiko (three weeks after Debora had abandoned house) to a hilarious welcome by Ndi and Mr. Ndeb. Upon arrival, he declared his willingness to become Ndi's next of kin. Ndi at once set *en marche rapide*, the machinery for the de-bastardization of Ngweh through the establishment of legal documents. He established a married certificate with Sophina in her absence, a birth certificate for Ngweh, and Letters of Administration proclaiming him next of kin. Then he went to church and offered mass for the deed. Then he asked one of his lawyers to take Ngweh round and show him his Tiko, Mutengene, Buea, Victoria and Douala warehouses and companies in which he had shares. After that, another lawyer took him round to show him the cocoa and rubber plantations in Mwenja and Dibonbare. Then another lawyer took him round to show him the hotels in Douala, Kumba, Buea, Victoria, Nkongsamba and Bamenda. After Ngweh had done the tours and seen what his father had as wealth, he invited Mr. Ndeb and told his father in his presence to hand-over the management of the estates to him for the simple reason that he wanted his father to receive treatment abroad.

"You can't be so rich and you have yourself treated in dispensaries in Cameroon – what you call hospitals. Are there any hospitals in Cameroon? It is not the appellation or infrastructure that is called hospital; it is the *savoir faire*, the expertise. At least, your life is still very valuable to me in particular and the rest of your family in general." Ngweh said.

"Who do you refer to as my family?" Ndi snapped.

"You, your three living wives, the eight girls and I are your immediate family."

"That's what you have come to teach me? How can divorced wives remain members of my family? I feel hurt."

"Let's leave that now. They are not your family. I am sorry. I would say your lawyers who should be more enlightened have done you a disservice. They would have advised you to seek medical intervention abroad. So, get ready to move to Europe. I have asked the lawyer in charge of your Douala businesses to prepare papers for your evacuation, hire a nurse who will take you to Europe, stay with you until you are treated and return with you. As soon as the papers are ready, you will leave. And I believe there should be no more debate on this."

Mr. Ndeb batted eyes at Ndi, Ndi batted eyes at Mr. Ndeb. Mr. Ndeb gasped and exploded absentmindedly, "Decree number one."

Ndi, seized by a fit of apoplexy exclaimed, "Won't that be a terrible waste of too much money!"

"A waste of too much money! What is money meant for if it won't save the only thing man cannot duplicate - life? Dad, your proceeds from the building materials you supplied for the construction of the Bonaberi Bridge cannot be exhausted within my life time if each member of your family spent a hundred thousand francs a day. So let's use part of it on you yourself and try to put you on your feet wholly or partially," Ngweh suggested.

Ndi withered instantaneously from the thought of having to lose so much money. Money should be hoarded and not spent carelessly. Furthermore, was Ngweh devising a way of devouring his money in his absence? Had he commissioned his wealth in safe hands?

Mr. Ndeb recovered from his absentmindedness and supported Ngweh's suggestion that his father be evacuated to a renowned hospital in Britain. He took some of the blame for not advocating evacuation when the accidents occurred. With Mr. Ndeb on Ngweh's side, Ndi had no choice but to wait for the evacuation papers. While waiting, Ngweh asked his father to make a will. Ndi trembled at the thought of making a will. He recalled his encounter with the matron. She had insisted that he made a will before going to the theatre. He had protested and gone to the theatre without one and returned from it safe. Won't it be wise to go to Europe without making a will? He reasoned.

"Is making a will the alternative of going to Europe? Can't I go without making a will?" Ndi asked.

"What's the problem with you? You have already made your will by making me your next of kin. What I expect from you now is to tell me where you would like to be buried and what should happen to your dispersed family if you died either in Europe or here. Don't mistake me for this. I am not sending you to Europe for death but for treatment. And take note everybody dies. Death is the ultimate end of all living things. And living things die everywhere at anytime. That's all."

"If I die, I should be buried here in my compound – here in Likumba. As for what you call my dispersed family, if I die shall I be there to know what happens to them? Shan't they be rejoicing that death had fulfilled their evil wishes? Is there one of them that has not contributed to my demise?" he asked with a tint of anger.

"That's all I needed from you."

Two weeks later the evacuation papers were ready and Ndi was airborne for the University of Glasgow Teaching Hospital where he spent six months in the intensive care unit and one year six months proximity recovery and training to use special crutches in a rented apartment.

While Ndi was away, Ngweh studied the family history very carefully. His father's parents had migrated from their village and settled in Mankon where they bought a large piece of land and built on it. Soon after, they begot Ndi the lone son of a six daughter family. The girls were all comfortably married. Apart from the new road that had taken part of the compound, it was still impressively large. Ndi had moved down south to Tiko to work as a labourer and had had very little contact with his family in Mankon. In fact, he took Tiko for his home. His parents' deaths were non-events since he was still wallowing in poverty. His parents' compound was given to a caretaker from his first wife's side in her presence. So, she knew the boundaries very well. Ndi became wealthy as a result of engineers overestimating the cost of government building projects, Ndi oversupplying building materials and selling and sharing the leftover with the engineers. In spite of his impressive wealth, he had very little investments in Bamenda. He hardly even talked about Bamenda.

The first project Ngweh undertook then was to build a two story building, cement his father's parents' graves, and fence the plot in Mankon. After that, he extended the building at Likumba by buying more of the adjacent land, building a chalet and making other modification on the old structures and fencing and cementing the compound. He drained the neighbourhood and improved on the access roads around the compound. He then embarked on tracing the whereabouts of Ndi's first wife. After several futile searches, he finally discovered her selling groundnuts in the Bambui market. He introduced himself to her and went and saw where she was living. He told her not to move house until he came back to Bamenda again. He would come purposely to install her where she belonged. Upon his return from Bamenda, Ngweh turned his attention on his father's third wife and her daughters. He discovered them in Tole Tea Estate. They were assisting their maternal relative in doing the mean job of harvesting tea but they were fine. He then went to Mundoni to find out about Debora.

Unfortunately, he discovered that her mother had forced her into marrying a Douala-based businessman but her daughter was left behind with her. He then went looking for Ndi's first daughter and discovered that her husband had had an accident and his leg had been amputated. Thus she had become the main breadwinner. By the time Ndi returned, Ngweh had developed a solid mental picture of what he expected the Ndi clan to be. To consolidate himself, he got married to a Bamenda girl of his father's tribe.

Ngweh's getting married in his father's absence drew drawn brows from many quarters especially Mr. Ndeb. He condemned all the projects and trips Ngweh carried out as blatant wastes of money, disrespect for a dying father and a sign of on-coming disaster.

"No doubt, he hurriedly bundled the old man out of Tiko to Europe. He wanted the leeway for a spending spree," Mr. Ndeb told one of his neighbours.

"*Massa*, I have never seen such extravagance, such uppishness, such superciliousness. What does he want to show us? Look at the cleaning project he undertook – cleaning the brook that forms the natural boundary between the Senior Service Quarters (SSQ) and ghettos, digging toilets for the ghetto fellows and filling potholes in the ghettos. The fellow just throws his father's wealth to the dogs. He does not care to ask for advice. He simply does things on his own," Mr. Ndeb's neighbour responded.

"I am making a catalogue of what he is doing. Everyday he goes to Bamenda to play life with women – Bamenda that his father never talked about. He has become more Bamenda than Bamenda people. If his father returns, I shall tell him without mincing words that if he does not harness that boy he will ruin the financial empire he has painstakingly built over the years," Mr. Ndeb said.

"Many people are against what he is doing. Since he does not seek advice, and he does not even go near people, nobody cares about him also,"

"Can you imagine that he spites even me who brought him from his village dungeon? Whatever goldmine he sits on today is of my making. But let me tell you, that boy does not care whether I am there or not. Before his father left this country, he entrusted him into my hands. But I am non-existent to him," Mr. Ndeb said, hit his foot on the ground and left the place with a promise to tell Ndi upon his return to reconsider his relation with Ngweh.

Chapter Twenty Five

Ndi returned to Tiko to a hilarious welcome. Ngweh had organized dance groups to welcome him at the Tiko airport and hired a special open-top car which drove him slowly among the dancing groups dramatizing the triumphant return to his house. When he got to his compound, he did not recognize it. He thought he was being received in a hotel newly built close to his house. The driveway from the main road was cemented, there a concrete fence, nearly all neighbouring houses were painted, the brook separating the SSQ and squatters' sharks was cleared and drained, the main building in the fence was renovated beyond expectation – its windows enlarged, the veranda completely tiled, toilet facilities improved with the three master bedrooms having each its own toilet etc.

When the last guest had returned, Ndi expected to be taken to his house. He told Ngweh he was tired and wanted to sleep and should be taken to his house.

"This is your house. We have just carried out some renovation on it," Ngweh said and led his father to his room. Ndi scanned the building in disbelief. He half admired and half condemned the artistry. It was too sophisticated for his liking. Agreed, he had seen more sophisticated artistry in Europe but that was Europe. In the cacophony of welcome, he did not take note that Mr. Ndeb was conspicuously absent. In the morning, he asked Ngweh whether he had seen Mr. Ndeb since his return.

"I don't think I saw him myself. One has been too busy to take note of every person. I believe he was there."

"You only believe he was there? That's surprising. Please call him for me."

Ngweh sent for Mr. Ndeb. On his arrival, he shook hands with Ngweh with the rigidity of robots. Ndi suspected that there was some strained cordiality but made no comments. "I wonder whether I saw you yesterday either at the airport or here at home. I believe I did not. What happened?" Ndi asked.

"I have not been feeling well these days," Mr. Ndeb responded, feigning illness.

"How could my reception be such a success then?"

"Ah, ah, Ngweh could do it alone and he really did and it succeeded."

"So how are you? How is Tiko? I am glad to be home. The white man has worked wonders on me. *Massa* we die in this country in vain. The white man knows medicine and works. Can you imagine that the services our nurses render patients here as if they were doing them favours, white nurses render them as the integral part of their responsibility? I believe if I had been evacuated on time, I would have recovered wholly. Unfortunately, as the Doctor told me, I came when irreparable damage had been done. So, though you see me standing erect, I am staked with a waistband," Ndi said and lifted up his shirt to show Mr. Ndeb the waistband. When he however turned to see whether Mr. Ndeb was appreciating what he was saying, he discovered that his eyes were cast somewhere else and his mind, a thousand kilometres away. He took offence and stopped talking. After a brief while, Mr. Ndeb feigned a call from his house and returned. Ndi concluded that there was a serious rift between him and Ngweh.

Three weeks after the return of Ndi, Ngweh went to Bamenda to supervise the finishing touches of the cementing of the compound. When Mr. Ndeb got wind of it, he went to see Ndi. "I have come to see you and break open my gall bladder before you. Your son Ngweh, has filled my bowels with water – Ndongo water. The last time I came here I fell short of refusing to come. What that your son has done, *hiim, hiim*. What is in the mind, the mouth cannot express. Nobody will tell you. You will see it yourself or you have already seen or been told. I did not want to start. And I shall not start. That is what has brought me. Good bye," Mr. Ndeb said and stood up to go.

"What have you said? Is that what made you leave your house? I believe you have something to tell me. Tell me and shame the devil instead of saying somebody else will tell me."

"OK, I should be frank with you. There is a proverb that, 'One's most hopeful trap never catches an animal'. I believe your son Ngweh would be like that. I don't believe that your wealth is safe in his hands. That boy squanders money like groundnuts. Can you imagine how much money that boy has thrown away since you left this country and even upon your return? I have never seen such extravagance, such carelessness, such pomposity. To cut a long story short, see the ghettos opposite this SSQ – millions of francs have been wasted clearing and draining this stream, millions have been wasted building toilets in the ghettos and filling potholes there, everyday, Ngweh is in Bamenda. What he does there nobody can tell. All I know is that he is squandering your wealth with girls. Can you imagine his uppishness – he gets married in your absence? Fortunately, since he does his things without seeking advice, he did not invite me. I only heard that he paid bride price on a girl and took her. Since women follow nothing but money the girl just came. Somebody told me that he saw him at Mundoni. What did he go to do there? As I say again, what is in my mind, my mouth cannot express."

Ndi made a tunnel view of the matter screwed his face and after a sinister and ominous inhalation, dismissed Mr. Ndeb with an implied promise that he would go into action

129

immediately Ngweh returned. Mr. Ndeb got the gist of it. He knew he had implanted the venom in Ndi and he would strike immediately Ngweh returned from Bamenda. And true to prediction, immediately Ngweh returned, his father, without waiting for him to take off his travelling clothes, picked on him, castigating him for wasting his money on unprofitable renovation of the compound, clearing the stream which formed the natural boundary between the rich and the poor, building toilets in the ghettos, moving up and down and squandering money, and getting married without permission.

Ngweh went to his chalet, changed clothes and after bathing, met his fuming father at the veranda. He sat down beside him and greeted him with no sign of anger. Ndi looked up at him but did not respond to his greetings. Ngweh left him and went and ate. After eating he met him again and said, "Papa, your son goes on a long journey, he returns safely, instead of being happy that he has returned safely you start scolding him for wasting your money? You went only to Douala – a stone's throw from here, and you nearly died in an accident. See, from your first hand experience, see how dangerous travelling is. Travelling endangers life. People don't travel for the pleasure of it; they travel because of the imperatives of life. Money can only save life as it has saved yours. It cannot buy life. And when I talk of money saving life, I mean money well spent. There is a difference between spending money well and wasting money. Spending money well saves life directly or indirectly. Wasting money destroys life directly or indirectly. Of all those things you accuse me of having done can you tell me on which side they fall – the side of saving life or the side of destroying life?

Ndi cast a venomous look at the speaker and asked for coffee – a strange habit he had brought from Europe. Ngweh looked at him sip the coffee and smiled. "Papa, it is boiling hot here in Tiko, but see, you are drinking coffee. Your trip

130

to Europe has not only prolonged your life, it has also made you have new values for it. Wonderful! The money spent on you was not wasted, it was well spent."

"It is not coffee I am talking about. I am talking about your broadcasting my money as if you were sowing grain," Ndi intercepted.

"Papa, I have told you that money is not the primary thing. Welcome your tired son then, and let him have the warmth of coming home safely. Show that he means more to you than money."

"OK, welcome."

"Thank you papa. Let me now have the warmth of my wife too before I come for us to discuss," Ngweh said and moved to hug his embarrassed wife.

Chapter Twenty Six

Good, papa you have accused me of several wrongdoings. I would say I might have done things some people do not appreciate. But I believe that the people who told you about the wrongdoings are ignorant of the things I have done and I am doing. Before I go on, I should tell you that I am a master of my convictions. I believe that whatever I have done is correct and I have neither regrets nor apologies to offer anybody.

On the question of my getting married without your permission; I decided to get married in your absence the day I heard that your situation was improving and you would return to this country alive. So, it became imperative for me to marry so as to insure a steady source of food for you and me upon your return. I did not see it proper to be buying food from the club as we did before you left. Secondly, I thought a General Manager of big establishments like yours had to look more mature and respectable by having a wife to cater for guests. And finally, I thought it would be pleasing to you to see your grandchildren by your dream heir. A sick person, especially an evacuated one is like a cracked glass. Its lifespan is not certain. So, I had to speculate on how long you would live again. I did not blow up the marriage. I simply paid bride price to have authority over the woman. Other formalities await your approval and execution.

On the question of clearing and draining the boundary some people of the SSQ would be pleased to see remain as permanent as the stream itself; I did it as a way of showing that the ghettos around you, Pah Ndi, have a special privilege for having you nearby. Not all ghettos have the privilege of bordering SSQ. These have to, so to speak, enjoy what other unfortunate ghettos cannot enjoy. Here too, we must look at it the other way. If you see how you got into wealth, you will see that the boundary between being wealthy and being poor is permeable and not a stonewall as some people would have liked. It changes unpredictably with time. And why should someone who was a ghetto dweller yesterday but skipped the boundary today not give glory to God by being charitable and extending a hand of fellowship to ghetto dwellers? Furthermore, if the neighbouring ghettos are well catered for, their ills in terms of pests, air and waterborne diseases and vandalism won't affect the inhabitants of the SSQ. Have you not taken note that the ghetto people no longer defecate in the stream? What about the mosquitoes? Many people say ever since the stream was drained there has been a drastic reduction in mosquitoes, and therefore a drastic reduction in cases of malaria. The other day, some ghetto men undertook to clear the stream of new sludge. They have at least learnt that cleanliness is everybody's concern.

On the question of moving up and down squandering your money; I would say, I did, and I am doing a lot of travelling to trace my sisters and their mothers – what I call your dispersed family. I traced your first wife selling groundnuts in Bambui market. I traced your third wife and her daughters picking tea in Tole. I traced your first daughter in Bimbia. Her husband had had an accident. His right leg was amputated. His wife, your daughter, is now the main breadwinner. I went to Mundoni to trace Debora. I met her daughter but was told Debora herself was married to a Douala-based businessman. I have been going to Bamenda and will go again next week. If you were strong enough I would have liked you to accompany me there. I have recuperated your father's compound and I am constructing your homestead there.

Now, papa, listen … (Ngweh shuddered and suddenly went limp with built up emotions. His father saw him wither within a second. He looked terribly shrunken and rumpled. Ndi gasped, and encouraged him to go on.) One thing that destroys man is manning other people's businesses. The people who implanted in you the venom you poured on me when I returned tired and worn out from a long journey are vile and unacceptable. Though I kept quiet, I was and I am still very unhappy with your approach. See, the only person God created and asked him to create me is you. You created me in my mother's womb in your image and likeness; that is why I resemble you. In your absence, I have no other person as a reference. As you created me in your image and likeness in the womb of a woman you were not married to, my mother; that is how you created my sisters in your own image and likeness in the wombs of the women you were married to – their respective mothers. If any of my sisters swears by her mother, she swears by her individual mother. But if any of them swears by her father, she swears by you, our common denominator. My going to look for them, where they are and how they are doing cannot be considered waste of time and money. They are as part and parcel of you as I am. The same percentage of your blood flows in them as it flows in me. In going to find out about them I did not require permission from anybody. I did not have to tell any person. I feel I am, because they are. And they must feel they are because I am. And we all must feel we are because you are. And so, you must feel you are because we all are. I am proud of my sisters. They must be proud of me. We have a common stock – you. When I shall succeed in bringing my sisters together, we shall build the Ndi clan – your clan. Your money in Douala and anywhere in the world cannot build the Ndi clan, only we, your blood children can."

Ndi experienced a terrible bang in his brain. He thought Ngweh had heard it. The house tended to whirl with him. He grinned and breathed rather fast. At last he asked Ngweh when he said he would be going to Bamenda. Ngweh said it would be Tuesday next week, five days off.

"OK, I shall go with you," Ndi promised without responding to Ngweh's defence.

Chapter Twenty Seven

On Tuesday Ndi and Ngweh left for Bamenda. Because of intermittent stops to ease up the old man, they got there late when most of the nearby hotels had been booked. When Ngweh thought of going to a distant hotel, his father suggested that they go and pass the night with an old friend instead of going to waste money in a hotel. Ngweh refused going to inconvenience a family that was not expecting strangers. They finally got two rooms in a Mission rest house. The next morning, they went to their compound under construction. Because the new road had transformed the place, Ndi could not recognize his childhood compound. Furthermore, the place had been bulldozed and flattened. And with the imposing story building that replaced his father's native huts, the face of the place had changed considerably. When Ndi got in and saw the cementing, he thought his son was showing him around somebody else's building site until Ngweh held his hand and started showing him the work in progress. "Here are the two graves of your parents, this is your father's, and this is your mother's. I cemented them to give them the reverence they deserve. You see, they are not raised to avoid giving the compound a sepulchral aura. Here beside your father's grave, I think, if you die before me, you will be buried. You are not a Bakweri man, and so, I cannot bury you in Likumba. When you are buried here, we, your children would make pilgrimages every year to the homestead or shrine of our ancestors — you and your parents lying here. You see this open courtyard, it is meant to handle large crowds for such ceremonies.

Along the eastern wall, I intend to build chalets for my sisters and their children so that when they come here, they should have a place to live in comfort and not go and spend the night with old friends or in hotels. Each and every one of us should be proud of a home, a place of reference, a place by which we can swear by our parents and grandparents when taking concerted action against the challenges of the world. The work of this rallying place, this El Dorado of the Ndi clan required constant supervision and so I came to Bamenda nearly twice every month. It is now at the final stage. Now let's go to the main building. This story building has 16 rooms. It is envisaged to cater for a growing clan for the next ten to twenty years. With chalets along the eastern wall, we shall boast of about thirty rooms. Your room is the first room on the ground floor. Because of your state of health I prefer you to occupy it. I keep praying that God gives you long life to have the pleasure of having a night in it one day."

One of the workers overheard Ngweh and intercepted, "Patron, two rooms are ready for use. We carried out the instructions you gave us last time you came here. We sent for rough-surfaced toilet tiles from Bafousam and completed papa's toilet too. Everything is OK, you can come and see."

"By Jove, and we went and passed the night in a hotel! That's fine. We shall therefore spend more time with you here than we thought," Ngweh jubilated and told his father he would have to go to Bambui to see his father's first wife. Ndi sulked but gave him the go ahead with a shrug of the shoulders. Ngweh returned from Bambui in very high spirits.

"Papa," he addressed his father, "It is amazing that Mama Balbina has accepted to come and take charge of this compound once it is completed. She had earlier resisted the idea. If she is installed here, she would be the mother of the home shrine – the hostess of honour whenever we come here. Your compound in Likumba would be the shrine of the Diaspora where we shall be converging to discuss the annual celebrations at the home shrine. I intend to install your third wife with her unmarried daughters there. She would be the mother of the shrine of the Diaspora. You see at the far end of this wall facing the road, I have made provision for Mama Balbina to sell her groundnuts as a pastime rather than a business for subsistence. Since she is obsessed with groundnut selling, she would do it and at the same time receive a monthly allowance to upgrade her upkeep."

"And your mother, where shall she be mother of a shrine?" Ndi asked.

"She is mother of her father's shrine in Bakossi. She is OK. I have given her the store I had and she is very comfortable."

"You want us to spend some extra days in Bamenda in what you call a shrine – an un-inaugurated shrine; don't you think that will be going contrary to native norms and customs?"

"The day I cemented the graves, I made a small *salaka* for the living and the dead. I bought two huge rams, killed one, had the women of this quarter prepare food, I bought wine and invited the elders of this quarter. Before they were served the food, I told them about your ill health and asked them to pour libations for the ancestors of this quarter to assist the Doctors treating you. Or if it were your time to return to eternity, your ancestors should bless and hasten the building of this edifice in which your next of kin would bring your body and lay it in state and after the physical honours granted you, you would be buried among your people. After the occasion, I gave them the live ram to kill and share. Each of them carried home a good chunk of mutton. Every indication is that your ancestors heard their prayer. All went well with you and the work is progressing normally. If you don't mind, I can invite them to chat with us over a bottle of whisky this evening and tell them that you have returned safely. Or, since we are no longer under the pressure of hotel bills, we can extend our stay and have a more elaborate *salaka*."

"I think that is the best thing to do. I was born here and grew up here. It won't be nice that after decades of absence, I come here and return without seeing the people with whom I grew up. Some are dead, but I have to see those that are living."

"OK, that makes it even better. I'll go to town and make the necessary arrangements," Ngweh said and went to town. He arranged with a hotel for food and drinks the next day. Then he bought a live calf. The next day the people came and were overjoyed at the reception Ndi gave them. After feasting, Ngweh told his father to tell the people to take the calf and kill it and share it at their convenience. Ndi's countenance changed as he thought the *salaka* had been blown out of proportion. Ngweh understood the meaning of the sudden change in countenance but encouraged his father to do as he had suggested. With a drawn voice, Ndi told the people to kill the calf and share. Ngweh reminded the sharer not to forget the widows. The people gave Ndi a standing ovation for the offer and did what they had been told to do. They wished Ndi and his son ancestral and God's blessings.

Chapter Twenty Eight

The next day, Ndi and Ngweh set off for their return to Tiko. After covering a long distance in silence, Ngweh broke the silence.

"We are returning from Bamenda, 100% your birthplace and about 50% mine. You have seen the work in progress, you have slept in the building but you have made no comments so far. I don't know your impressions. I am saying this because we are getting near Mr. Tchamkouncheu's shrine. You will see the marvel of architectural triumph. It is the talk of this area. Mr. Tchamkouncheu was a very rich Bamileke Douala-based businessman who died without a hut in his village. When his children brought his remains at home for burial, the villagers drove them and showed them…aha! that is the monument, I shall like us to go there. The villagers drove them and showed them where once lived a kin group by the name Tchamkouncheu. They said they had never known of any person from their village living in Douala by that name. So, by virtue of a name reminiscent of Tchamkouncheu they showed them the hillock on which a Tchamkoucheu kin group once lived; where, you see, that monument is standing. Mr. Tchamkouncheu's children then went and buried their father there, there in the bush without ceremony. That place was all bushes at the time. The houses you see there now came after. Although some of the offended children advocated taking the corpse back to Douala for burial in their massive compound, the next of kin preferred burying his father in an eternal place, a place of reference, a place they would forever call home. To shut up their father's critics in the village, they built that edifice that now lords and graces not only his grave but the whole village. Every five years, Mr. Tchamkouncheu's children from all over the world come to the shrine and celebrate his life in pomp."

"Who told you all that?"

"The man who took me to Bamenda for the first time I went there to find out about your family. After him several other people told me the same story."

"Mr. Tchamkouncheu's children built a shrine after his death not before his death. They wasted money for their own glory. Whatever they do there now has nothing to do with their father," Ndi said with a betraying tint of anger.

"Agreed. They built a shrine after his death. But it was to counter the disgrace of his and their lack of foresight. I don't want us to be like them. I am building a shrine to enhance your image. We need not move from disgrace to grace as they did. This reminds me of what your first wife told me. She said you are in the habit of keeping valuable things. For example you bought a lot of cutlery from some retiring CDC white senior cadre but you have hidden the cutlery ever since. You are hiding them for whom? Dead people don't eat with cutlery. When will you use them? When you have a party, show the people what you have. Get some of the cutlery and use it on daily basis. That is living. You must have the feel for your wealth and let the population have it as well."

"If I don't use them shan't you use?"

"Use them and I shall use them after you have used them, that is what is called 'inheriting something'. You bought from the white man – that is not inheriting. That is trade. You buy to use, use, and I and my sisters shall inherit."

"OK, let me sleep. We shall discuss when we get home."

"I won't recommend sleep on a bumpy road like this. This part of the road is very bad and a sudden bump into a pothole of stone would affect a sleeping person more. Let's converse till we get to a smoother section."

"You go on then. I am listening."

"Yes, we were discussing Mr. Tchamkouncheu. You see, the value of what we did in Mankon cannot be measured in terms of money units. That act of charity provided meat for widows who might not have had the opportunity of eating meat for a long time. It has given them pleasure and prolonged their lives – lives that have no duplicates. That means it was not a waste of money but the appropriate use of money. By that act of charity people who did not know you, have now had the feel of your wealth. They will pray for you and wish you well. Mr. Tchamkouncheu never went to his village, let alone, gave a helping hand to the needy. His piles and piles of money in banks were of no consequence in his death. See the scorn and contempt with which mere natives treated his corpse. By your act of charity, you have sloughed that sleazy human weakness. You have made yourself great."

"Political figures look for greatness. Business people look for money. I am a businessman. I am very sensitive in the use of money."

"Yes, when we talk of piles and piles of money, we are talking of the superfluous. Superfluity is not the essence of life. It kills at both ends – the miserly and the extravagant."

"OK, I think the road is smooth now. Let me sleep."

Ngweh allowed his father sleep till they got home. After four days, he told his father that it was imperative for him to go to Bakossi and see his mother. He said she needed guidance especially as some people would want to abuse his absence and rundown her business. Immediately he left Mr. Ndeb got wind of his departure and visited Ndi.

"Mr. Ndi, I am afraid, you may mistake my caution for spite. I try as much as possible to avoid your next of kin because I don't want to be caught in your family disputes. I told you upon your return from abroad that Ngweh was not the boy I thought he was. You went out with him for days.

You have observed him. You can judge for yourself whether he is ideal or not. I am just an observer. If he is good, maintain him. If he is not, do something now that you are still living. That is what I have come to tell you."

"Ngweh is like spittle in the mouth. You can't spit him out completely nor shallow him completely. What I saw him do in Bamenda has dumfounded me. He has built a marvellous compound which he calls a Ndi shrine. There he says I shall be buried close to my parents. He says I am not a Bakweri man and he won't bury me here in Likumba. What annoys me about him is that all that I hate and have divorced, he is integrating. He has gone to fetch my first wife and reconciled with her. He says he is going to make her the mother of the Mankon shrine. He says he is going to bring all my daughters together and insure that each of them is well placed. He says this compound is the Ndi shrine of the Diaspora. It would be the rallying place for them of the Diaspora, and my third wife would be its mother. His philosophy is too sophisticated for me. One thing I have taken note of him is that he does not drink, does not smoke, and does not run after women. He is very discreet in doing things and has wonderful human touch. Because of that, he is highly admired by his workers. They readily carry out his instructions even in his absence. But he talks too much."

Mr. Ndeb lost a heart beat. He exhaled loudly and left without bidding Ndi goodbye.

Chapter Twenty Nine

Ngweh stayed three weeks with his mother before returning to Tiko. Upon his return, his father gave him a hearty welcome. He asked him how his mother felt when she saw him, whether she was missing him and how she was doing.

"She is doing fine although she is in constant dispute with people who accuse her of giving in to your demand that I move town. The people say you have no claims over me because you did not marry her," Ngweh said.

"So, what was their reaction when they saw you? Did they try to convince you not to come to me? If they did, what did you tell them?" Ndi asked with a trembling voice.

"I told them that I was a river that forked out in the dry season and therefore capable of supplying both branches with water,"

"What does that mean? I don't seem to understand," Ndi complained.

"A river that forks out in the dry season does so at its convenience and apportions water equitably to the branches. None of the branches dries up. But a river that forks out in the raining season does so under pressure and creates the main and the subsidiary branch. In the dry season, the subsidiary branch dries up."

"So your mother knows that you are not gone for ever? How is her business?" Ndi asked.

I think she is doing well because I had dismantled the huddles she would have encountered."

"How did you do that?" Ndi asked.

"In the villages the greatest problem with small businesses especially retail provision stores is borrowing. I neutralized borrowers by writing in front of my store, "Borrowing Is Not Cumulative", and made borrowers sign for having borrowed. When my mother took over from me, all the people who had borrowed but had not paid back and wanted to borrow again, she showed them that they still owed and as such they could not borrow. Nobody insists. So, she is fine."

"That is good. You think when we increase her capital she will be OK?" Ndi asked.

"She would. But the capital should not be disproportionate with her needs,"

"OK, I see. You are always cautious. Now tell me, I admire the projects you are undertaking. They cost a lot of money. Where do you take the money?" Ndi asked.

"I got money from the proceeds of the different business units, paid the workers and used the left over. I did not touch the capital. To ensure the healthy life of a business unit, only the proceeds should be used in non-profit making projects like non-commercial buildings. For example, when I started the small business in my maternal village, I used the first year's proceeds as a security against borrowing. I lent out only to the tune of the proceeds and not above. So the proceeds became the flyingwheel between the customers and the store."

Good. You said when we were returning from Bamenda that I did not comment on what you are doing. I could not, because most of what you do is contrary to what I would have liked you to do. You integrate what I divorce. You value what I disvalue. Your world view is completely opposed to mine. Why that difference if as you say I created you in your mother's womb in my own image and likeness?" Ndi asked.

"It is because we have two different value systems, perhaps brought about by differences in upbringing and the changing times. You were brought up by both parents. I was brought up by one. You divorced your wives either because they did not reproduce or because they did not beget sons. You forgot that you took after your father who begot seven of you, six daughters and you, the lone son. Like your father, you have begotten nine of us, eight daughters and a lone son, me. You consider the daughters valueless because you think they cannot be next of kin – this is tradition-based reasoning. I consider them of very high value because they can be next of kin. My mother is. This is the way things are now. Furthermore, suppose you were so rich and you begot neither son nor daughter, what would happen to your wealth upon your death? It would surely be inherited by a distant relative – brother or cousin. In the same vein, suppose you were so rich and you had only a daughter, what would happen to your wealth in this prejudiced system if you died? It would surely be inherited by somebody who is not as blood-close to you as your daughter. So, you see, man's value systems work contrary to those of nature.

Another thing I shall point out is what you call 'waste of money'. You have only two systems in terms of the use of money. Your money is well spent or well used if it is ploughed back into business; and badly used if it is used to give pleasure or save life. I was scandalized that when I suggested that you be evacuated for medical attention, you screamed that it would be a terrible waste of money. If you could say that on what concerned you, what would you say on what concerns somebody else? Now see, do you know how happy I am to have a father talk to me? Can money replace what we are doing, this face to face, father and son conversation? Do you know what it means for a child to be deprived of the love of a father or mother? The fact that I hadn't a father when I needed one most makes me ecstatic having one now. That was perhaps the mystical force that propelled me to suggesting that you receive medical attention in the most efficient hospital. I wanted to buy a rare opportunity and thank God, I succeeded.

In relation to the use of money, money used to save life or give pleasure is not money wasted. It becomes money wasted only if there is superfluity. As I said, superfluity is the abuse people make and call it enjoyment. When a person drinks and falls in the gutter, and says 'Lo! we enjoyed ourselves yesterday,' can we say he is in his right senses? No, we can't because that is the wrong side of enjoyment, it kills."

"I see in your plan the possibility of infusing my lineage with unwanted bastards. By this I mean, when you take all those unmarried sisters and make them procreate here to form what you call the Ndi clan, they will bring all textures of blood into the lineage. Since you are alone, their blood would overwhelm the genuine Ndi blood and very soon the clan will lose being a genuine Ndi clan and become a nondescript one in terms of blood granule. When that happens, you'll see children with marked differences in physical appearance, character and general disposition. You see strange faces adulterate the family hue, the family name becomes a common denominator for a 'confederation of neighbourhoods', something gets missing," Ndi said with poignant concern.

"There again Papa, man's value systems work contrary to those of nature. The word bastard is one of those language weevils that play havoc on the user rather than on the supposed referent. People use it sardonically to distinguish what they consider pure blood from alien blood. Nature does not do that distinction. Nature distinguishes between worth and worthlessness – a worthy person (man or woman) and a worthless person (man or woman). From personal experience many people use the word to pick on others in a

148

bid to humiliate them. For example, in my maternal Bakossi village people call me bastard. But let me tell you, my mother told me that her father was a very prominent and prosperous man. But because he was distraught by the syndrome of not having a male heir he became careless, in fact, he squandered all that he had and by the time he died he was virtually a beggar. His male relatives knowing that inheriting his position at any level would yield them no benefit, and taking into cognizance that his death celebration would entail a lot of expenditure, sort of created broken-bridge relation with him while he was still alive. In fact, they sort of 'scoffed' the right of inheritance at my mother. Upon his death, they expected nothing from her. But my mother, with my support, carried out a no-nonsense convention-challenging ceremony – one that has not been equalled till date. While distracters were incredulous about the source of her strength, the chief who knew the truth hailed me. When it came to who would inherit my grandfather's chair in the Ahon society, the chief suggested that I be made his successor. The pure-blood advocates shouted that they would prefer a woman, my mother, to a bastard. But tradition holds that only men can be members of the Ahon society. So in the impasse they chose one distant cousin of my grandfather. When my mother tried to protest, I hushed her down. The day the fellow was to be installed he bought bonga; and of course, since the society does not eat bonga, they sent for me. I refused being reconsidered but gave the fellow a pig to give to the society. Till date the chief of the village has great respect for me. There is no single pure-blood in that village who does not owe me. I am not very versed in the Bible. But from the little I know, good and evil co-exist and man evolves in their co-existence. In their co-existence they supersede each other at both the individual and collective levels. Adam and Eve fell at the collective level; Cain fell at the individual level; Sodom and

149

Gomorrah fell at the collective level; Job rose at the individual level; Christ rose at the collective level and so on. Even in families dominated by sons, alien blood infiltrates at different times and degrees. So, the desire for pure-blood remains the prerogative of fate. In other words, man is helpless. Man's wishes are not the determining factor."

"Do you know what made me divorce those women? If you were to integrate them in your plan, you would have sought my permission. Why did you not?"

"Papa, a next of kin is proclaimed on the dying bed. And in most cases the patient dies. In your case, I was proclaimed next of kin when it was still possible to redeem you. So I thought I could still fight to restore your life, and of course, glory be to God, there you are. So, our case is very different from other cases. I could not wait for you to die. Though your life was in the balance, I speculated on getting the better from uncertainties and I got, while at the same time going on with the demands of next of kin. May I also add that I thought what made you divorce your wives was tradition-based reasoning – reasoning that blames the woman for the misfortunes of the world and so sidelines her; forgetting that she is the vessel of creation and the hub of wellbeing. In my perspectives, I thought you separated with your wives and you could be reconciled even posthumously. For, look at it this way, could you dichotomize between wishful thinking and problem-solving in divorcing your wives? Think of your age, your odyssey in marriages and your helplessness in the face of reality. And of course, you would agree with me that you could not change your situation by divorcing your wives. So, I thought, if you died, your wives and daughters would be given the recognition they deserve."

"Now that I am alive, what do you advice?"

"I want you to toe the line in recognizing the woman as an inevitable partner with full rights in all aspects of life; whether she bears children or not; and whether she bears sons or not. The first step then is for you to assemble your whole family, reconcile with them and plan to inaugurate the shrine in Bamenda and after that, the shrine in the Diaspora. You will reconcile with all your people and prepare them for the yearly celebration of your life."

"I am old and sick. The task is yours. Whatever you say, shall be done. Come forth then, and knee down, and let me commission you to the task ahead." Ndi requested.

Ngweh moved to where his father sat and knelt down. Ndi placed both hands on his son's head and rolled them down to his knees and back to the head and said: "You are Ngweh; and I hear the name means in Bakossi, counsellor. So, counsellor, as you say I created you in your mother's womb in my image and likeness and created also your sisters in their mothers' wombs in my image and likeness, I am happy to declare that you have recreated my mind in your mind's image and likeness. As you think of the woman, so do I think of her as from today. Where you place her, there I place her. Don't falter; bring your sisters and their mothers together and make me have 'salvation' in them. By placing my hands upon your head I make you the head of my family. Bring them together as you have promised. I give you unequivocal powers to carry out your desire. And in this, be blessed that I may be blessed.

151

Chapter Thirty

Ngweh stood up, thanked and embraced his father and said to him, "Papa, you have set fire on my head. I accept to do as you have commissioned me. And I must set to work right away."

The next day, Ngweh went to Douala and got a service transport vehicle and sent it to collect his father's third wife and her daughters from Tole. When they came he introduced them to his wife, and told his wife that his father's third wife, who would be known as from then as small-big mami, was the mother of the Likumba compound. She was the hostess of honour in charge of receiving the other members of the family for that come-together and the subsequent ones. But because she had been away for some time, his wife would temporarily assume her functions while small-big mami got acquainted with the compound.

Ngweh had made accommodation easy. He had maintained the first and third wives in their respective rooms in the renovated main building, had converted the firewood kitchen into a large self-contained chalet for the daughters with the intension of having them together and making them get used to each other, and had built for himself and his wife, a suite on the newly acquired land. Two days after the arrival of the small-big mami and her daughters, he sent the vehicle to Bamenda to bring the first wife – big-big mami. And a day after her arrival, he sent for Ndi's first daughter and her two children a boy and a girl. He then went to Mundoni himself for Debora's daughter.

When everybody was in place, he invited a photographer for a family photograph. He placed Ndi in the middle and made him carry Debora's daughter while his grandchildren by his first daughter sat in-between his legs. Then on Ndi's right hand he placed big-big mami, and on the left he placed small-big mami. He then arranged his sisters according to their heights. Finally, he and his eldest sister, Ndi's first daughter took the back row.

After the photograph, the family sat to have their first meal together. For the first time since he became a financial magnate Ndi found himself fully engaged in another sphere of life. He was so elated that he hugged his daughters and caressed his wives and tried to tell several dry stories to dispel the web of guilt that still fettered his mind. His wives reciprocated with chilling cynicism. Whenever he threw in a flat joke, they blew up the laughter. At one point, Debora's daughter wriggled out of his hands and as she ran to his first daughter, she fell, hitting her nose on a stool. "O! My daughter is dead!" Ndi exclaimed with raised hands. Big-big mami and small-big mami batted eyes at each other. They could not believe what they were seeing. They clapped their hands simultaneously to express surprise at Ndi's concern for a daughter. Ngweh dashed for the child. "Bring her here," Ndi requested and asked whether she was hurt. "She's OK. She's always running," Ngweh said, cuddled the child for some time then gave her to Ndi. The child continued crying. The big-big mami got up and got her from her father and soothed her to silence.

"O child; that you were to be silent in my hands for always!" the big-big mami said rather spontaneously.

"Nobody instructed her," Ndi chipped in.

Ngweh jumped in with, "That is what has brought us here. And I think we must now know why we have assembled here. I shall give the floor to papa to tell us why we are gathered together. Papa the floor is yours."

154

"I cannot give you the floor and you give me the floor. Go on. Tell your mothers and your sisters why we are gathered here today. I am sick. I can die at any time. So, go on, Ndi responded.

"OK, Papa, big-big mami and small-big mami, my sisters, I thank God that by His grace we are able to gather here today. I should have been strange to you if when I set out in search of you, I did not introduce myself to you and tell you I was not happy with the way we were dispersed. I said I wanted us to come back into the Ndi fold as his wives and children. Today is the blessed day when my dream has come true. You had all lived in this compound before. Only little Cecilia and I can say we are strangers here. But all of you expressed surprise with the changes that have taken place here. Big-big mami could not recognize her room. The children could not recognize the veranda in which they had played everyday. Why this? It is because of renovation, sloughing the old and acquiring the new. If you look around, you will see that the ghettos have been cleaned and that there is no longer pungent smell coming from the faeces and sludge in the stream. You see, this compound has been enclosed with a concrete wall. Papa could not recognize his compound when he returned from Europe. Why? Of course, because the compound was renovated. So, all around us is symbolic of what has brought us together. We have to renovate our minds and bodies in order to slough our old selves so that the people who knew us will be unable to recognize us in words and deeds. We have to be enclosed in the Ndi new spirit as this wall encloses all the buildings in this compound. And we have also to extend a hand of fellowship to the outside world as we extended in cleaning the ghettos. I know this will not be easy because the causes of our dispersal laid in us pungent sediments of the past – sediments which if we want to express, will definitely turn into bombshells. It is not how far we express our rights and wrongs that matters but how far we can contain them. If I could speak for everybody, I would say that we better not say anything. Let each person just shame the devil with silence."

"I think that is the best thing to do," Ndi echoed.

"My son Ngweh, when you met me in Bambui market for the first time I was sceptical about your proposal. But when I kept receiving your encouragement, I thought I should give you a try. I am a plantain stem, I don't blunt a knife. I am the chairwoman of the St. Theresia Movement in the Bambui Parish, I stand for the truth," big-big mami said.

"Where the needle passes, there the thread passes," small-big mami also said.

"Thank God that the two of you who are the most aggrieved have decided to keep quiet about the past," Ngweh said and looked round to see if the girls had something to say. None of them raised her hand. Ngweh turned to his father. "Papa, anything to say?"

"What do I say? What can I say that would make the situation better? Go on. The only thing I can say is that you go to the cow fence and buy a proverbial bull for my family and tomorrow, celebrate this great day, a day I shall never forget. I am so elated!"

"You have said it! You have crowned it!" Ngweh exalted with raised hands.

"Wooooooooo!" the rest of the family echoed and started singing and dancing. The people of the SSQ heard the singing and dancing and rushed to join in. The people of the ghetto heard the singing and dancing, and ran in to sing and dance. The entire neighbourhood heard the singing and dancing and jumped in to sing and dance. The whole of Tiko heard the singing and dancing and joined in to sing and dance, and so they danced and danced, and danced to celebrate the Ndi clan. What a next of kin!

Titles by *Langaa* RPCIG